Ever since she showed up at his house in that maid's uniform...

It had gotten extremely uncomfortable to be around him!

Sheyna didn't know what had gotten into her that day except to say that she hated to lose. She knew the skimpy outfit would get Jace's attention, and just knowing Jace wanted her gave her a rush.

But when she fell into his arms, Sheyna never expected Jace to scoop her up and cradle her close to his chest. Now, no matter how hard she tried, she couldn't forget the hungry look in his eyes. Even now, closing her eyes, she saw his chocolate face only inches from hers, and his sexy, dark, bedroom eyes.

Just thinking about Jace was enough to heat her blood again. Sheyna sighed heavily and faced reality. She was sexually attracted to her childhood friend and boss. *But there was no way in the world she would ever let Jace Beaumont know how she really felt about him!*

Books by Angie Daniels

Kimani Romance

The Second Time Around
The Playboy's Proposition

ANGIE DANIELS

is an award-winning author of twelve works of fiction. A chronic daydreamer, she knew early on that someday she wanted to create page-turning stories of love and adventure. Born in Chicago, Angie has spent the past twenty years residing in and around Missouri, and considers the state her home. Angie holds a master's in human resource management. For more on this author you can visit her Web site at www.angiedaniels.com.

the
PLAYBOY'S
PROPOSITION

ANGIE
DANIELS

KIMANI™
ROMANCE

KIMANI PRESS™

ISBN-13: 978-0-373-86053-1
ISBN-10:   0-373-86053-6

THE PLAYBOY'S PROPOSITION

Hello Readers,

Welcome back to Sheraton Beach, Delaware, where the people are friendly, the beaches fabulous and the men sizzling hot!

I want to thank all of you for your e-mails, letting me know how much you enjoyed *The Second Time Around,* Jabarie and Brenna's story. I listened to all of your requests and it brings me great pleasure to introduce you to Jace and Sheyna.

Feisty Sheyna Simmons has never backed down from a challenge, so when Jace Beaumont propositions her to surrender to him—mind, body and soul—for forty-eight hours, she accepts. After one unforgettable weekend, neither of them will ever be the same again.

I had a lot of fun writing this book. So kick off your shoes and get ready for another trip to the beach.

Enjoy,

Angie Daniels

Cherie Belcher of Missouri and Louise Brown of Georgia, this book's for you.

Prologue

Jace Beaumont was ready to pummel whoever was ringing his doorbell. He stomped down the hall of his lavish town house, mumbling all kinds of four-letter words. "I'm coming. Hold your horses!" he yelled at the top of his lungs. Opening the door to a gorgeous woman, "*damn*" was all he could muster.

"Hey," Sheyna Simmons said in a sexy voice as she struck a dramatic pose.

His eyes traveled to a figure-hugging maid's uniform, which included a white apron and headpiece, then slid lower to a pair of incredibly long legs. They lingered there long enough for him to wonder how those legs would feel wrapped around his waist, before he wisely diverted his attention to back to the smirk on her face. "Sheyna...what are you doing here?"

The mahogany beauty blinked, then looked surprised that he had even asked that question. "What does it look like?" Sheyna brushed past him and tottered into the foyer on what had to be four-inch stilettos. As soon as Jace closed the door and turned around, she smiled and held up a spray bottle in one hand and a squeegee in another. "I've come to wash your windows."

For a long moment, Jace struggled to make sense of her words. He thought he'd misunderstood and prayed he had, but the look on her slender face told him otherwise. "You're serious, aren't you?"

Sheyna stared at him as if he had two heads. "Hey, we had a deal and I'm here to honor that. Now, where do you want me to start?"

He eyed her cautiously. The ability to breathe was suddenly as difficult as was believing this was really happening.

Two days ago, they had played a game of volleyball and, as naturally competitive as the two of them were, he had challenged her. The loser had to come to clean the winner's house windows while wearing an apron. Glancing down at the cleavage spilling over the top of Sheyna's uniform, Jace swallowed, then answered in a low voice, "I guess you can start in the living room."

Her heels made distinct clicking sounds as she made

her way across the oak flooring to a floor-to-ceiling window. Stopping in the middle of the room, she spread her legs into a wide stance and took a moment to simply look out at the ocean, drifting onto the sandy shore outside. While Jace took in her appearance from behind, pleasure clenched his stomach. Gone was the conservatively dressed woman who worked beside him in the office. In her place was this beautifully erotic goddess. Swallowing, he had a strong feeling that this was one challenge he was not going to win.

"Do you have a step stool?"

Sheyna's voice drew his attention back to her face as she looked at him innocently over her shoulder. He groaned inwardly. Sheyna was baiting him and, as good as she looked, all he could do was grind his teeth and pray for the strength to resist.

"Yep, I have a stepladder in the closet." Jace stepped out of the living room and moved to the end of the hall, glad for a few moments away to get his resistance in place. He drew in a ragged breath then reached inside the closet, removed the small ladder and carried it back to the living room.

"Thank you," Sheyna said, and leaned over slightly, the low cut of her bodice giving him a bird's-eye view. It didn't take a rocket scientist to know she wasn't wearing a bra. *Oh, boy, this is not going to be easy.*

Hands buried in his pockets, all Jace could do was

watch as Sheyna carried the ladder over to the window then sprayed cleaner on the glass. He shook his head in awe. He'd never seen Sheyna in anything sexy. Also, she'd never filled out her clothes quite the way she did today. If she had, he hadn't noticed. He shouldn't be noticing now, but she looked too good to ignore.

Swinging around, Sheyna caught him staring and frowned. "Why don't you quit staring and go get me a roll of paper towels?"

"Sure."

Embarrassed, Jace quickly turned on his heels and moved to the kitchen, feeling like an errand boy. Once there, he dropped down at the small table and took a moment to catch his breath. He felt intoxicated. Nothing could have prepared him for Sheyna showing up at his doorstep dressed like that. He had made the bet in fun and certainly hadn't expected her to even show up, let alone in uniform. But she had, and the resulting desire that coursed through his body was like nothing he'd ever encountered before. He had always been attracted to her, but this went beyond the normal scope of things, and he could honestly say he never felt this level of attraction for a woman. Yet, it was there and now he was wondering what he should do about it.

"Did you forget about me in here?" Sheyna called from the living room, breaking into his thoughts.

Jace jumped from the chair and removed a roll of

paper towels from the supply cabinet then strolled back into the living room to find her standing on the ladder. He froze. The back of her skirt was so short he could almost see the cheeks of her… His body reacted predictably. He had a strong desire to carry her to bed and fight out the storm that had been brewing between them for months.

"Jace!"

He felt as if he was in a hypnotic trance and forced his eyes to focus on the frown on her face. "Here you go." Stepping forward, he handed her the paper towels then immediately backed away.

"It's too quiet in here. Why don't you do me a favor and turn on a little music," she suggested softly.

"Sure." He walked over to the solid-oak entertainment center that took up the entire left wall and hit the play button on the CD player. A slow R & B tune floated across the room and Sheyna started swaying her hips to the beat of the music, stirring up all kinds of wants and needs that he had no business having. His Adam's apple lodged in his throat as he watched her. Never had he imagined the smallest movement could be so damn enticing. God, she was good. *Too good.* He shifted his weight to his other leg. What the hell was she up to?

While she worked, Jace let his eyes wander where his hands could not and quickly decided Sheyna had to be the sexiest woman he'd ever encountered. The stilettos lifted her heels high off the ladder step, making her toned legs look incredibly sexy. Sheer black hose covered those shapely legs up to her thighs, where a skimpy garter belt met them. Using his imagination, he envisioned that beneath the short skirt she was wearing a thong or an itty-bitty G-string.

Jace mentally jerked himself back from going there and decided to spend his time trying to figure out what she was up to. Because he knew damn well it was all a game.

At the Beaumont Corporation, he was the boss and she was a part of his team, but this evening, Sheyna was in control. She was running things. She was holding his attention in the palm of her hand, and with the sway of her generous hips, she could have him begging.

And she knows it.

It was a game they had been playing for years. He groaned inwardly. Both were equally competitive and always needed to be in control. Neither wanted to lose. It was one thing when they'd been kids fighting over a game of kick ball, but now they were all grown up with adult needs and wants and the stakes had changed. *Really changed,* he thought as he couldn't resist another look at her in the seductive uniform.

Jace stood, leaning back on his heels as he studied her soft curves. Her movements were making him hard and weak. He needed to leave the room, but he couldn't get his feet to move. *What is going on?* She was his friend, and yet in the last several months he had been feeling things that he would never have expected to feel for his buddy Sheyna Simmons. Recently, it was as if she knew the power and effect she had over him and was playing with him just to see how far she could go. He could tease her all he wanted, but lately, he could rarely get a rise out of her. Even now, she was like the expensive art in his parents' curio cabinet, he could look but couldn't touch. Frustrated, he couldn't wait a moment longer to ask the question that was burning in his brain, "You're getting a big kick out of this, aren't you?"

Turning, Sheyna gave him an innocent look. "I have no idea what you're talking about. If anyone should be getting a kick out of this, it should be you. After all, I'm here washing your windows, not the other way around." She tore off a paper towel, wiped the window and watched him out of the corner of her eye. "Don't you have some work to do?"

She knew him too well. He guessed that's what happened when you've known someone most of your life. He just hoped she didn't realize that the sight of her standing in his house, in that sexy costume, reminded him she was all woman and he was very much a man who, right now, was horny as hell.

"Yeah, I'm reviewing candidates for the general manager's position."

"Then go do your job and let me do mine." With that

said, she swung around and started humming to the music, ignoring him.

Irritated, Jace quietly turned on his heels and moved to his office on the other side of the kitchen.

For the next half hour, he tried to concentrate on a stack of résumés sitting on the desk in front of him and tried to forget about the woman who looked like a pin-up model working in the other room but the heat settled at his groin wouldn't go away. He couldn't work. All he wanted to do was go back down the hall and watch her work.

He turned on a small circular fan, hoping the cool air would help clear his head of his inappropriate thoughts. His brain scrambled to make sense of what was going on. He and Sheyna were friends, not to mention he was her boss. So why weren't his mental and physical barriers in place? He had to keep reminding himself that Sheyna Simmons was off-limits, but for some hormonal reason his body wasn't listening.

Jace struggled through the depths of his thoughts and returned to reality enough to concentrate on the résumés in front of him. The general manager of the Beaumont Hotel in Virginia Beach was leaving in less than two months to work with Disney World Vacations. After conducting a nationwide search, Jace had yet to find a candidate who had the leadership abilities the position required.

He had almost managed to shift his brain elsewhere when he heard a crash and Sheyna's scream. Springing from the chair, he hurried down the hall and found her in his bedroom, the ladder on its side, and Sheyna on the floor.

"Are you okay?" he asked, his voice dripping with worry as he swept her, weightless, into his arms and carried her over to his bed, lowering her onto his lap. He examined her with a concerned gaze.

She nodded and took a deep breath. "Yeah, I leaned over too far and I guess I lost my balance."

His hand slid up her arm. "We can't have that. You want everyone to think I'm abusing you?" he teased.

Sheyna pressed a hand to his chest and offered a weak smile at his attempt at humor. "Everybody already knows you're a slave driver."

They shared a laugh and then he sobered quickly when he realized how close they were. He had her in his room. On his bed. On his lap. Sheyna looked at him and their eyes connected. Despite the fact he knew this was a bad idea, he couldn't move, not with her curled so close to him, her sweet scent reaching inside his senses, tormenting him. It was too easy to get lost in the way she looked. As much as he knew it was dangerous, he turned his head toward hers, their mouths only inches away. She looked so vulnerable with her lips slightly parted. He leaned forward, but before he could kiss her, she turned away. Sheyna suddenly struggled to her feet.

"Well, other than your office, I guess my job here is done," she commented while avoiding eye contact.

Staring up at her, all Jace could do was nod. "Thanks for cleaning my windows."

"You're welcome," she returned with a sugary smile, then, with an exaggerated sway, she sashayed across his room and out the front door.

As Sheyna moved down the sidewalk toward her car, a triumphant smile curled her lips. Jace may have won the game but she had won the battle. Hopefully, he'd think twice before ever challenging her again, she thought with a chuckle as she climbed into her car and drove away.

Chapter 1

Six months later

An attraction to her boss was one thing Sheyna Simmons refused to admit to.

No way. No how.

It would completely contradict all the years she'd spent telling her best friend, Brenna Gathers, she couldn't stand him. Admitting her feelings would also jeopardize the strong working relationship that had taken the last seven years to build. Yet, for some reason, as she stood on the other side of the ballroom, she couldn't remember any of those things. Maybe it had something to do with his dark sable eyes or how sexy he looked in a black tuxedo with red accessories. Or maybe, she thought with a scowl, the feelings had managed to push past her protective wall because of the gorgeous little starlet he had draped on his arm. Whatever it was, she hoped she figured it out, because being attracted to Jace Beaumont was not even an option.

Sheyna brought the fruit punch to her lips and forced her eyes over toward the gazebo, where the bride and groom were posing for a professional photographer, and smiled, glad for the distraction. Brenna Gathers Beaumont was a glorious vision in white.

Family and friends had gathered in the Princess Ballroom of the Beaumont Hotel to celebrate the wedding of Jace's brother, Jabarie Beaumont, to Sheyna's best friend, Brenna Gathers. Sheyna had served as the maid of honor while Jace had been the best man.

"I think this wedding is the event of the year!"

Sheyna looked over at Brenna's aunt, Nellie Gathers, who also stood in as Sheyna's mother on occasion, and nodded. "I agree. You and Jabarie's mother did a fabulous job."

The Beaumonts had spared no expense. An elegant candlelight wedding at Mount Hope Baptist Church had been filled with their rich friends and family. Afterward, the wedding party had been escorted to the beachfront hotel in four white stretch limousines. Ice sculptures, live jazz music and an abundance of red and white roses adorned the room. Nothing less for the heir of the Beaumont Corporation.

"We did do a fabulous job, didn't we?" Nellie replied, then added with a laugh, "Now it's time to work on getting you married."

Chuckling, Sheyna leaned down toward the woman who was almost a foot shorter than her five-foot-nine-inch frame and replied, "When you find him, let me know." Smiling, her eyes traveled to the floor where the bride and groom had moved out to share their first dance as husband and wife. Sheyna watched with envy as her best friend gazed up into the eyes of the only man she had ever loved.

Sheyna heaved a heavy sigh. Sure, she would love to find Mr. Right. Although she wasn't looking, Sheyna hoped someday to fall in love with that special man she would spend the rest of her life with. Preferably, long before her biological clock started ticking. But since she wouldn't turn thirty until her next birthday, love was the last thing on her mind. Instead, she was all about having a little fun.

"I think the perfect man is standing over on the other side of the room."

Sheyna followed the direction of Ms. Nellie's eyes and drew back slightly. "You aren't talking about Jace, are you?"

"Of course I am," she replied, her chestnut eyes shining with approval.

"Puhleeze," Sheyna snorted rudely. "I wouldn't marry him if he were the last man on earth."

Ms. Nellie made tsk sounds with her tounge. "Never say never."

Never was putting it mildly. Jace was a heartbreaker, and Sheyna had sense enough not to become another notch on his headboard. "Ms. Nellie, trust me. Jace is used to women falling all over him, which puts him on my uh-uh list." Besides, he was overbearing and cocky and it was because of him she kept a bottle of ibuprofen on her desk at work. Sure, Jace was handsome with dark eyes that rarely revealed his innermost feelings, but he was a love 'em and leave 'em kind of guy, which made him all wrong for her.

"Well, being good-looking and rich does sometimes cause a man's head to blow up."

"Blow up? Jace's head exploded a long time ago," Sheyna said with a chuckle, and Ms. Nellie joined in.

"We can't fault the man for having something women like."

No, she didn't fault him, but that didn't mean she liked it. Growing up, Sheyna had fallen under that type of spell more than once. She'd had her heart broken on several occasions when she had been foolish enough to think she'd found Mr. Right. She knew she was as susceptible as the next sistah, and, as a result, she'd learned to stay away from men dripping with charisma and sex appeal—such as Jace.

Sheyna couldn't resist gazing across the room again. "Ms. Nellie, Jace is nothing like Jabarie. His secretary spends more time taking messages from his women than typing his letters."

"Shame on you, starting rumors," Nellie scolded.

"It's true." As the director of human resources for the Beaumont Corporation, Jace was as aggressive as any headhunter when it came to filling key positions, which meant he was used to getting what he wanted.

Well, so was she. As the only girl raised by a father and two overly protective brothers, she'd grown up the baby with three men doting on her and giving her everything she wanted.

"Who's that on his arm?"

Sheyna glanced briefly at the nutmeg beauty by his side and snorted rudely. "His flavor of the month."

Nellie looked at Sheyna closely and started laughing. "I think I hear jealousy."

Sheyna gave her a skeptical look. "Ms. Nellie, did it ever occur to you that maybe Jace isn't my type?" There were some women who were immune to men like him.

"Well, you're obviously his type because here he comes."

The song changed to Jagged Edge's "Walked Out of Heaven," and her stomach quivered and turned as she watched Jace move across the dance floor in her direction. He moved toward her with a grace that caused heat to travel down between her thighs. Jace had that determined look in his eyes and she felt her heart rate increase in immediate expectation. Suddenly, Sheyna wanted to storm out of the hotel and keep running until she was far away from him and the feelings he stirred at the pit of her stomach. For goodness' sake, they were friends and being attracted to a friend was not allowed.

As Jace drew closer, Sheyna could feel his aura even from where she stood. *Get a grip!* She scowled, then self-consciously reached up and smoothed her short tapered hair. Okay, so she wasn't even going to try to pretend he wasn't fine. Uh-uh. Jace was definitely eye candy. Tall, with wide shoulders and a body that made a woman stand and pay attention.

"Hello, Ms. Nellie," he greeted, then moved in to kiss the older woman gently on her smooth caramel cheek.

"Hello, Jace. You look so handsome today. I hope you came over here to ask Sheyna to dance?"

Her head snapped around to glare at Ms. Nellie.

"I sure did," he said with a smile, then shifted his gaze to Sheyna. "May I have this dance?"

Sheyna looked over at him then rolled her eyes. "Why aren't you over there dancing with Ms. Boob Job?"

"Because I'm asking you," he retorted. Deciding not to wait for a response that wasn't coming, he grabbed her hand and led her out onto the dance floor.

At the center of the floor, Jace rested his hand at the

small of her back and pulled her close then moved to the beat of the music. "See, that wasn't so bad," he muttered near her ear. Pulling back slightly, he gazed down with a gleam in his sable eyes that made her want to do something she was certain she would regret later.

"Just be quiet and dance," she mumbled angrily, then wrapped her arms around his neck. His cologne filled her senses, and she smiled. She had bought the subtle blend for him for Christmas last year. She'd known it would be perfect. Obviously, Jace agreed because he'd been wearing it ever since.

Glancing over his shoulder, Sheyna spotted his date standing near the ice sculpture with her hands planted at her hips, looking directly at them. She didn't look happy. *Good.*

Jace moved his hand across her back. Sheyna's skin tingled and caused her nipples to harden beneath the strapless red dress.

"Where's Jaime?" he asked.

Jace was one of the few people Sheyna could be totally honest with. "I dumped him last week when he suddenly remembered he was married."

"Ouch!" he replied, while she laughed bitterly. "I didn't like him anyway." Sheyna pulled back, and before she could retort, Jace cut in. "Hey, he didn't deserve you. Sheyna, hell, the last three dudes didn't, either. Face it, your taste in men sucks."

She lifted her chin. "And yours doesn't?"

His eyes danced with mischief. "I don't date men."

Her lips turned downward. "You know what I mean."

Shrugging, he pulled her close and the hair at her nape moved beneath the whisper of his breath and another sensation stirred in her abdomen. "It really doesn't matter. None of them ever make it past the three-week mark."

"Oh, yes, how could I forget," she mumbled. Jace ended relationships before there could be any emotional attachment.

"Poor Jace. He has it so hard," she singsonged. "How much time does Ms. Boobs have left?"

"Her name is Carren Clark and she's a columnist for the *Sheraton Beach Tribune*."

"I didn't ask you for her résumé. I asked how much time she had left."

"A week," he replied around a sigh.

"Pity."

"Why?"

"I think your mama likes this one," she said as she watched Jessica Beaumont standing beside the beauty, engaging her in a conversation.

"That's because Carren's grandmother is a good friend of hers."

"Oh, of course," she muttered, her voice dripping with sarcasm.

His mother was one tough cookie. Her scheming had

kept Brenna and Jabarie apart for five years. Jessica thought Brenna could never be good enough for her son and did everything she could to sabotage the couple. Luckily, she came around and, in the end, welcomed Brenna to the family with open arms.

"You know good and well I've never cared what my mother thought of my dates."

Sheyna leaned back and barked, "Liar. If we were dating your mother would have a cow."

"Why don't we try it and find out?" he said, with that familiar challenge in his eyes.

That dark gaze roamed over her face and lowered to her mouth and still lower over her bare shoulders. Jace was studying her like a man interested in a woman. She shivered and turned away, not wanting him to see so deeply inside her. "I've got better things to do with my time."

"Why are you shivering?" he probed.

She snorted rudely. "Because it's a little chilly in here."

Jace chuckled and his breath on her skin sent goose bumps down her arm. "I thought maybe I had that kind of effect on you."

"In your dreams," she snapped. The song ended and she pulled away from his grasp. "Now, go play with your little girlfriend." She turned and moved over to mingle with some of the other guests while she waited for her heart rate to return to normal.

An hour later, the bride and groom were getting ready

to leave. Sheyna moved through the crowd in search of Brenna and found her standing to the far right. She walked over to say goodbye and hugged her best friend.

"Thanks for everything." Tears sparkled in Brenna's hazel eyes.

"Girl, you know it ain't nothing I won't do for you. Have fun in Aruba."

"I plan on it. I'll see you in two weeks."

Sheyna grabbed a small bottle and as the couple left she joined in the fun of blowing bubbles at the newlyweds, then she watched as they climbed into one of the limousines and headed to the airport. As soon as the car was out of sight she went ahead and said her goodbyes then moved to the coat check to retrieve her wrap.

"Leaving already?"

Swinging around, her lips turned in a wide smile for Jaden Beaumont.

"Yeah, it's been a long weekend."

His long locks brushed the shoulders of his tuxedo as he moved to help her with her wrap.

"When are you heading back to California?" she asked.

"The day after tomorrow."

She nodded knowingly. The youngest of the Beaumont brothers was probably anxious to return home.

Roger Beaumont had taught his children they could have or do anything they wanted as long as it involved the Beaumont Corporation. Another career field was never an option. Jabarie and Jace had followed in his footsteps, while Jaden, the black sheep of the family and the younger brother, had taken off shortly after graduation to find his own way. He was the only one who'd ever stood up to their parents and she admired him for that. "Let's have lunch tomorrow," she suggested as an afterthought.

His grin widened. "Sounds like a plan."

Jaden escorted her to her silver sports car. Sheyna waved then pulled out of the employee parking lot of the hotel. It was well after eight o'clock and fog curled around the coastal roads. Reaching up she turned on her windshield wipers. Inside the ballroom she had forgotten about the drizzling rain that had been falling all day.

While obeying the 35-mile-an-hour speed limit, her eyes traveled up and down the wide cobblestone streets lined with single-story buildings and mom-and-pop stores. Sheraton Beach, a waterfront town with a population of less than five thousand residents, was the only home she'd ever known or loved.

Yawning, Sheyna was anxious to get home and curl up beneath her sheets. Helping Brenna for her wedding had been draining and she was glad it was over.

Fifteen minutes later, Sheyna stepped inside her house, tossed her car keys onto a small table and locked the door behind her.

Home at last.

Plush beige carpet silenced her steps as she walked

down the hall to the first room on the right. Sliding her
purse off her shoulder she lowered it and herself onto
the bed and finally removed the shoes from her sore feet
with a sigh of relief. She wore high heels on a regular
basis but the Prada pumps that Mrs. Beaumont had insisted the wedding party wear were uncomfortable.

Damn that woman and her son.

Sheyna scowled for even wasting another second
thinking about him. Sighing, she reached up and
rubbed her temples with her fingertips as if doing so
would erase Jace from her mind. Being around Jace
shouldn't be as hard as it was. She saw him Monday
through Friday and sometimes weekends, and she
should be used to seeing him. Yet, in the last several
months it had gotten extremely uncomfortable to be
around him.

*Ever since you showed up at his house in that
maid's uniform.*

She didn't know what had gotten into her except that
she hated to lose. She knew the skimpy outfit would get
Jace's attention and the thought of making him lust for
something he couldn't have was too tempting to pass up.
Only, she'd never expected Jace to scoop her into his
arms and cradle her close to his chest when she fell from
the stepladder. And now, no matter how hard she tried,
she couldn't forget how good it had felt being held in
his arms or seeing the hungry look in his eyes. Even

now, closing her eyes, she saw his chocolate face and those dark bedroom eyes only inches from hers. She released a shaky breath. Nothing about their relationship, personal or professional, had ever been simple.

Opening her eyes, Sheyna rose and raised the window, welcoming the cool October air. She hoped it would cool the heat flowing through her veins. Within seconds she felt better, but it did nothing for the yearning that raged through her body. Usually, standing near the window staring out at the ocean made everything in her life better. That was one of the reasons why she loved Sheraton Beach and why she had bought a house within walking distance of the ocean. But Jace was one thing that wasn't easy to overcome.

Wrapping her arms around herself, she stared out at the leaves that had been scooped off the ground by a strong gust of wind. Fall was definitely upon their small town. Sheraton Beach was quiet. The Beaumont Hotel only had off-season guests who were taking advantage of the special rates. It was the best time of the year for the staff of the Beaumont Corporation to set aside work long enough for training and development. At least that's what she had been trying to get Jace to understand. He was so stubborn that most days she wanted to give her boss a swift kick in the butt.

Just thinking about Jace was enough to heat her blood again. Sheyna sighed heavily and faced reality.

She was sexually attracted to her childhood friend and boss. Yet there was no way in the world he could ever know how she really felt about him.

Somehow, she was going to have to find a way to get past her feelings before they jeopardized everything she had worked so hard to accomplish.

Chapter 2

Jace woke up the next day with the morning sunlight filtering through a gap in the curtains and a scowl on his face. He had tossed and turned and he blamed his restless night and erotic dreams on one person.

Sheyna Simmons.

He swore under his breath then rolled onto his back and folded his arms behind his head as the previous evening came flooding back.

After the wedding he had planned to end the night at Carren's place, but that had been before he'd seen Sheyna promenade down the aisle of the church in the soft red sleeveless dress that complemented her dark skin. He remembered his mouth going dry as he appreciatively watched her move, the light bouncing off the highlights in her naturally wavy brown hair.

While standing at the altar beside his brother, he'd felt the overwhelming rush of intensity as she moved toward him that made him almost wish it were his wedding day.

At the ridiculous thought Jace flung the covers away from his body and lowered his feet to the floor. He couldn't understand what was happening to him lately. Getting married was one thing he had no intention of ever doing, which was why Carren had gotten pissed off.

After he had danced with Sheyna, he had returned to Carren, still feeling the effect of their contact. Sheyna's alluring and exotic scent had wrapped around him and made him dizzy with an adrenaline rush. Even as he danced the next three songs with Carren, his mind was elsewhere and Carren knew it. He couldn't blame her for asking if he'd like a wedding similar to his brother's. When he froze and stared down at her flabbergasted, she put a hand to her hip and demanded to know where their relationship was headed. He had no choice but to tell her the truth. Nowhere. She sulked all the way to her house where he made sure she made it safely inside the door before he returned to his car and headed home.

He didn't like hurting women's feelings and breaking hearts but love just wasn't something he was interested in. Jace frowned as he remembered being in love once. She was beautiful, funny, smart, but Julia Edmonds was also disloyal and shallow. Happily ever after had not been in the cards for Julia and him.

After her, he doubted he was strong enough to endure the kind of pain loving and losing brought. Eventually he'd decided, what was the point? So to keep from falling into the love trap, he only dated women he wasn't at risk of falling in love with.

Rising, he moved into the adjoining bathroom and within minutes was beneath the spray of the water. Lowering his eyelids, all he could see was Sheyna in that long red dress. For some reason he was just as aroused as he had been when she had come to his town house in a skimpy maid's uniform.

Sheyna had the most amazing amber-colored eyes, a family similarity she shared with her father and one of her brothers. The way she pouted when she was mad about something she felt strongly about… The intense heat that flared her eyes… Those thickly lashed eyes could bring the right man to his knees. But he wasn't the right man for her and he knew it. Besides that, she was his friend, and more importantly, they worked together. Nevertheless, the last several months he'd found himself comparing all of his dates to Sheyna.

Jace looked forward to going to bat with her over issues she strongly believed in. He found himself wondering what it would feel like to have her be as passionate about him as she was about her job. He knew that was a dangerously foolish thought, but it was a thought just the same and one he felt was worth exploring.

Jace lathered his washcloth and decided it was time to think of something—or in this case, someone—else. Maybe he should have spent the night with Carren, but doing so would have left him irritated and unfulfilled because the only person he wanted to be with was Sheyna. What was happening to him? How in the world could he be attracted to Sheyna Simmons?

He dated lots of women and had a reputation for being a player. Jace had always dated women who looked good on his arm and only spoke when necessary, women who fawned over him and were willing to cater to his every need. But now that was not enough. There was no challenge. Those women no longer satisfied his taste. Maybe it was because whatever Jace wanted, those women willingly gave him with no ifs, ands or buts. But not Sheyna. She would tell him to fetch his own slippers and cook his own meal. A smile curled his lips. She was a pistol, and what had always irritated him about her he now found to be so damn sexy.

Damn her.

He didn't know what had gotten into him lately. Something must be wrong with him because in the past, if a feisty woman like Sheyna had approached him, he would have run the other way. But now things were different. He was different. Sleeping with beautiful women was no longer enough. He wanted and needed so much more.

But Sheyna? He shook his head. Not now, nor ever, could Sheyna be the woman for him. Nor would he ever think to approach her like a man interested in a woman. She was stubborn, opinionated and, most importantly, his coworker. No matter how attracted he was to her, he would never jeopardize their working relationship. She was the glue that held the department together with her exceptional employee-relations skills and her deep compassion for others. Nope. The best thing for him to do was ignore what he was feeling. He was sure it was just him wanting something that he knew he could never have and that in itself made her a challenge. But some things were better off left alone.

Just as he heard a knock at the bathroom door Jace climbed out of the shower and wrapped a towel around his waist.

"Come in," he called cheerfully, knowing good and well it was his brother Jaden, but he was surprised to see his baby sister, Bianca, stick her head in the door instead.

"Squirt, what are you doing here this early?"

"Came to hang out with Jaden. I made breakfast."

He stilled and sniffed. Sure enough, he smelled bacon. Jace smiled. "I'll be right out."

Bianca laughed, causing her curls to bounce around her round face. "I'll put your waffle on the griddle."

Five minutes later, in gray sweatpants and a white T-shirt, Jace strolled down the long oak hallway into the kitchen where his siblings were at the table eating.

Bianca smiled when he stepped through the door. "Perfect timing." She got up to take a golden-brown waffle off the griddle and carried it over on a plate.

"Thanks, squirt. You're the best." He kissed her honey-brown cheek then moved and took a seat across from Jaden who was feeding his face while reading the newspaper.

"Good morning," he mumbled between chews.

"Think you can pass me the syrup?"

Without looking up from the paper, Jaden slid the bottle over from his side of the table. Jace usually spent his mornings reading the paper while having breakfast. *Guess that isn't happening this morning.*

Bianca carried over two cups of hot coffee and set one in front of him, then took the seat beside him.

Jace gave her a long look. "Why is it the only time you make breakfast at my house is when this bozo breezes into town?"

"Because I know that bozo isn't getting a home-cooked meal," she replied, then reached over and playfully tugged one of Jaden's dreadlocks.

"True that," Jaden said with a wink.

Jace poured syrup over his waffle as he scowled. "Nobody told him to move all the way on the other side of the United States."

"You don't know what you're missing, either. The women in L.A. are gorgeous," Jaden began, then took a sip from his mug. "Have you slowed down any at work?"

"Never."

Jaden sighed with regret. "You know, I wish you'd take some time off and come and visit. When was the last time you took a vacation?"

A long time ago. He had wrapped his life around the corporation and took very little time for himself. "It's been a while."

Jaden scowled. "I know. I've been asking you to come to California for as long as I've been there. No wonder you can't keep a woman."

Jace released a bark of laughter. "You're kidding, right? I've got more women than I know what to do with."

Jaden had been living on the west coast for almost five years. Immediately following high school, he had escaped the clutches of their controlling parents and almost given their mother a heart attack when he joined the Marines. After a short tour of duty, he'd decided to stay in California and had opened his own body shop.

Jaden folded the paper in half and reached for his coffee mug again. "Actually, I'm thinking about coming back."

"What?" Bianca's eyes danced with excitement.

Jace looked into dark eyes identical to his own and waited for him to continue.

"I ran into Mr. Peterson yesterday and he told me he's planning to sell his shop next summer and he's willing to give me a good price." While Jaden was in high school, Mr. Peterson, who had never had any kids of his own, took the boy under his wing and taught him everything there was to know about fixing cars.

"Wow, it would be great to have you back," Jace said between chews.

"Oh, it would be perfect!" Bianca exclaimed.

Jace gave Jaden a strange look.

"What? Why are you looking at me like that?"

"Because I can't believe you finally decided to come back home."

He shrugged and brought a forkful of scrambled eggs to his mouth. "I missed being around family."

"And we miss you." Bianca sprung from her seat and hugged him close.

"Just don't say anything yet to Mother," Jaden warned. They all knew how much their parents disapproved of his chosen occupation.

"I won't," Bianca said.

"Yeah, right." Jace gave her a long hard look. His sister couldn't keep a secret. "You might as well put an ad in the newspaper."

"Ha-ha!" she barked, then reached for her coffee cup

and took a sip. "I know how to keep a secret, especially one this important." She looked at her brothers over the rim of her mug while her eyes danced with excitement. "What are you going to do with your shop in Cali?"

"I won't have any problems selling it."

Jace nodded. It would be nice having his baby brother home again. "The grease monkey is moving back."

Bianca bubbled. "Wait until Mother finds out. She's going to blow a gasket! Not that I'm going to tell her."

Jaden laughed. "Yeah, right." The siblings chuckled.

Jace brought a strip of bacon to his lips. "What do you have planned today?"

Jaden glanced across the table at his brother. "I'm going to drop by the shop after I have lunch with Sheyna."

Jace stilled. "Why are the two of you having lunch?" he asked, then realized how ridiculous that must have sounded.

Jaden smiled. "Because she invited me," he replied, then leaned back in the seat. "I guess she knows a catch when she sees one," he teased.

Jace struggled to keep his jealousy at bay. So what if they were having lunch together? His brother had known Sheyna as long as he had. Besides, Sheyna wasn't his, so his feelings were out of line. But knowing that didn't make it any easier, especially since his siblings were watching for his reaction.

"I guess I'd rather it be you than some of those other

cats she likes to date," he finally said, and brought a forkful of waffle to his mouth.

Jaden shook his head with ridicule. "Why do you hate the men she dates so much?"

As Jace chewed he realized it was more complicated than that. He didn't think any of the men she dated were worthy of Sheyna, but if he tried to explain that, people would read it wrong and make more of it than it really deserved. But ever since he'd seen her in that maid's uniform, he'd found himself wondering what lay beneath all that cotton and lace, and resenting any man who knew the answer. However, what bothered him most were the feelings that afternoon had conjured. Jace finally answered his brother. "Because she could do better."

"I'm sure she says the same thing about you."

"Me?" he said with a snort. "If you want to know the truth, I think she's in love with me and uses those men to try and make me jealous."

Bianca jumped in. "Oh, please! The last thing Sheyna needs is a workaholic. Believe me, she isn't interested."

"Yes, she is," he said jokingly. "I'm the most eligible man in Sheraton Beach."

Jaden chuckled. "Maybe now, but I'll be back soon and I'm taking that spot."

Jace shoveled eggs into his mouth and faked nonchalance. "Where are you planning to eat?"

"I thought we'd go to Spanky's."

Spanky's was voted as the best "first date" spot in the city. Good food. Dimly lit room. Live music.

He hesitated. "Actually, Sheyna and I have a few things to discuss. So, I think I'll join you." He tossed Jaden a look across the table. "Unless you have a problem with that?"

Bianca looked from one brother to the other and her smile deepened. "Sounds like a fabulous idea."

Jaden chuckled. "Squirt, I couldn't agree with you more."

Chapter 3

Sheyna pulled into the restaurant's parking lot, and as soon as she spotted the gray SUV with the license plate BEAU, her pulse jumped. She'd had no idea Jace was planning to join her and Jaden for lunch. Seeing him every day at work was bad enough, but during her free time…

After turning the car off, she leaned back in the seat and took a few minutes to calm her nerves. For years, she and Jace had spent hours hanging out at each other's houses, going to lunch and sometimes even enjoying a movie. Never once had she ever thought of him as anything more than just a good friend and another brother to add to the two she already had. But in the last year, long before she had showed up at his house to clean his windows, all that had changed. She couldn't pinpoint the exact moment, however, she could honestly say that, since the day she had cleaned his windows, the rhythm of their relationship had changed somehow. She'd started noticing things about Jace that she had never paid attention to before, and just being in proximity to him caused her hormones to rage out of control, which was why sitting at the same table with him for the next hour was going to be as difficult as hell.

The cowardly thing to do was to call Jaden from the parking lot and cancel lunch, but she'd barely had time to talk to him at the wedding and had been looking forward to spending some time with him before he headed back to California. Besides, she thought with a stubborn frown, since when did she run away from anything?

Since you realized you're attracted to Jace.

That may be true, but she would just have to get over it. Hopefully, during lunch, she could keep her emotions in check. The last thing she needed was for Jace to know she was foolish enough to become sexually aroused by his mere presence. She took five more minutes to get herself together before she finally took a deep breath and got out of the car.

Sheyna walked into Spanky's Bar and Grill and was immediately impressed. The color scheme was black and white. Large plants adorned the room and the smell of mouthwatering dishes flooded the air.

For a Sunday afternoon, the establishment was crowded. The restaurant was larger than she had envisioned from the outside. There were several dozen tables around the room, as well as booths along the walls. A bar was to the right. In the center was a small platform stage, which she was certain was utilized every Friday and Saturday night. According to a coworker, a live band played on weekends, although right now light jazz was coming from a large jukebox in the corner.

Before the hostess could greet her, Sheyna spotted Jaden waving from a booth toward the back. She moved in his direction, heart pounding, expecting to see Jace at any moment. However, when she rounded the corner, she was relieved to discover Jaden was alone.

He must have driven Jace's SUV, she thought by way of an explanation.

As she moved closer, his grin broadened. The Beaumont brothers looked so much alike. Same milk-chocolate coloring. Big sable eyes and lashes that any woman would die for. Women loved them and Sheyna could see why. They were all equally handsome. It was their attitudes that set them apart. Too bad she'd never felt anything romantic for Jaden, she thought as he rose to his full six foot three. She took in his athletic build in jeans and a Lakers' jersey. At twenty-five, Jaden was like a baby brother to her.

"Hi," she greeted him with a smile.

"Hey, you." Jaden leaned over and kissed Sheyna on the cheek before he motioned to the other side of the booth. "Have a seat."

"Thanks." She slid onto the seat and shrugged out of her denim jacket. "Have you ordered yet?"

Jaden shook his head. "No, we were waiting for you."

Before she could ask him to define *we,* Sheyna spotted Jace coming from the direction of the restrooms. She experienced that familiar curling sensation in her stomach. Her throat got tight, her thighs trembled. He looked good. Tall, dominant and as handsome as hell in loose-fitting jeans that hung comfortably on his hips, a red long-sleeved T-shirt and a red baseball cap. She loved to see a man wearing red. The way she was reacting, Jace was no exception.

"Hey," Jace greeted her with a smile that threatened to steal her heart away as his dark gaze raked over her.

"Hello," she managed nervously as her heart raced away a mile a minute at his closeness. "I didn't know you were joining us."

"I was hungry and decided I couldn't pass up a corned beef on rye." He then slid onto the bench beside her. "You don't mind, do you?"

"Why would I mind?" she asked, as if it was no big deal. However, just sitting next to Jace caused her body to remember what it had felt like being in his arms on the dance floor. Not that she was interested in him that way. They were just friends. She'd learned her lesson about dating men like him years ago. Taking a deep breath, she told herself the best thing for her to do was to ignore him.

Sheyna made a show of looking around the restaurant before her gaze shifted to Jace. "What, no bimbos on your arm? Where's your Barbie doll?"

"Probably with one of those toads you call a date," he countered, then laughed at Sheyna's offended expression.

Jace had the unique ability to challenge her at a level that made her want to taunt him. "Funny. At least the men I date have brains."

His mouth curved slightly and one fine dark eyebrow lifted, challenging her. "And that's not saying much. Didn't the last one forget to tell you he had a wife?"

Sheyna groaned and clenched her hands together in her lap to keep from socking him in the chest. "Remind me never to tell you anything again," she said, then pressed her lips tightly together.

There was a noticeable pause and Sheyna knew in that instant Jace regretted even saying anything. "Sorry," he mumbled, voice low and all humor erased.

It was her fault. He was so stuck on himself that she could never resist taunting him even if that competitive streak of his kept him from resisting and lashing back, and as a result, he put his foot in his mouth.

Sheyna knew his apology was sincere. In the past,

anything she told Jace he'd held in the strictest confidence, but she rolled her eyes anyway. As long as she was angry with him, she wouldn't have to worry about that funny feeling coming back. "I just bet you are." She then turned her attention to Jaden who dragged a hand down across his face.

"Can we enjoy one meal without the two of you getting into it?"

"That's him."

"That's her," Jace said at the same time, then cleared his throat and ignored Jaden's throaty laugh.

Sheyna folded her arms on the table.

Caught between them, Jaden rolled his eyes. "Maybe I need to leave the two of you alone."

"No!"

"Absolutely not." Sheyna slid as far away from Jace as she could. Jaden chuckled and seemed intrigued by the animosity that seemed to always have existed between them.

Sparring with Jace was always fun. Sheyna was starting to believe that it wasn't strictly competitive, not anymore. For her, she was battling against her attraction to him.

"Tell me, Jaden, how's California?" she asked, eager to change the subject.

"Great, but I'm starting to feel homesick."

"You? Homesick? That's a new one."

The waitress came by to take their order. When she left, Jaden leaned back in the padded seat of the booth and continued. "I was telling my big brother here, I'm seriously considering coming back and taking over Mr. Peterson's shop."

A cry of joy broke from her lips. "That's wonderful! I'm sure that will make your parents happy."

"I just bet it will," he replied, and they couldn't help laughing.

Sheyna knew his mother well enough to know she'd never cared much for having a mechanic in the family. She sipped her water. "You really want to leave California and come back to our little town? I find that hard to believe from someone who couldn't wait to graduate so he could get as far away from Sheraton Beach as possible."

He simply shrugged, his locks brushing his shoulders. "You can only run for so long. Being away has actually made me appreciate this place all the more. California is fast paced and expensive. Beaches aren't as accessible as they are here."

"I guess not. Here you have your own private beach," she joked. "The woes of being rich."

He gave her an uncomfortable grin. "It's not just that. I guess I just miss this place. Besides, I think it's time for the handsomest Beaumont brother to return to his roots."

Jace snorted rudely. "Yeah, right."

Sheyna giggled then reached for her glass and took

another sip of water. The two of them definitely had charisma.

Glancing over Jaden's head, she spotted a tall woman coming through the door. Sheyna waved and signaled for her to come over. As soon as the leggy beauty stopped in front of their booth, the brothers took one look at her and practically sprang from their seats.

"Hello," she greeted them as her cinnamon-colored eyes traveled from one brother to the next.

"Danica Dansforth, let me introduce you to two of Sheraton Beach's most eligible bachelors. Jace and Jaden Beaumont."

Jace was the first to hold out his hand. "It's a pleasure meeting you."

"The same here," she said as she took his proffered hand, then, as she released it, she turned her head and gazed up at Jaden and her smile widened. "Hello."

"Hello, to you," Jaden replied in a voice laced with husky sensuality. Sheyna watched as his eyes roved over Danica appreciatively. They stood for the longest time staring at each other before Sheyna cleared her throat. "She's one of my bachelorettes."

"Your what?" Jaden asked without taking his eyes from the tall beauty.

"For the charity auction I'm having Saturday."

"Really?" he drawled softly, giving her his full attention.

Every year Sheyna coordinated an event to raise money for the Sheraton Beach Youth Center. The nonprofit agency offered after-school programs for children in the community in an effort to keep them off the streets. The bachelorette auction was one event that had proved, three years running, to be quite popular. Not only was it for a good cause, but with all of the supporters in town, it always brought in large contributions. Thank goodness for the women who were willing to strut their stuff around the room while men bid for a dinner date with them. This year's headliner was going to include a weekend for two at the Beaumont Grand Chateau in Las Vegas with former runway model Danica Dansforth.

Danica batted her eyelashes and smiled sweetly. "Hope you can come on Saturday."

"I'll make it my business to come," Jaden said with a wolfish grin.

Jace cleared his throat around a chuckle. "Bro, I thought you were leaving on Friday?"

Jaden gave his brother an annoyed look then returned his eyes to Danica's smiling face. "I think that maybe I need to stick around at least until after the auction. Anything for a good cause."

Sheyna turned and exchanged a knowing look with Jace. Jaden was obviously attracted to the beauty. "Danica, why don't you join us for lunch?" she suggested since it was obvious Jaden was too in awe to realize he was being rude.

Danica shook her head, sending auburn curls bouncing around her face. "Oh, no. I wouldn't want to intrude."

"No, we would be delighted to have you. Wouldn't we, Jaden?" Sheyna asked, pushing him with her foot under the table.

"Huh?" he said, and turned startled eyes on her, having quite forgotten she and Jace were there. "Oh, yeah, we would love to have you."

Sheyna noticed Danica's expression revealed equal amounts of intrigue and appreciation. "Then I'd love to."

Jaden rose and moved aside so that she could lower herself onto the bench. As soon as she was seated, he sat beside her.

The waitress arrived with their food, then took Danica's order before moving to check on the couple at the next table.

"Jaden, Danica just retired from modeling and moved to Sheraton Beach."

"You did?" he asked, eyes sparking with interest. "What made you give up modeling?"

While Danica explained that after ten years she was ready to do something different with her life, Sheyna watched in amusement as Jaden hung on her every word.

Anyone could see why a man would be intrigued by

her. Danica was six feet tall, had shoulder-length auburn hair, skin the color of coffee with a splash of cream, high cheekbones and large, slanted eyes.

Sheyna was chewing on her grilled-chicken sandwich while still watching the couple when, from under the table, she felt Jace squeeze her knee.

"Get your hand off me," she hissed between clenched teeth as heat radiated up to her core.

Leaning over, Jace mumbled close to her ears. "Why do I get the feeling you set this up?"

Sheyna reached for a fry and tried to maintain a straight face while the warmth from his breath sent a tingle down her spine, curling her toes. Damn that man! She groaned inwardly. Jace had always been able to figure her out, which was one thing about him that drove her nuts, but it didn't drive her anywhere near as crazy as the feel of his hand on her knee. She pushed his hand away and immediately felt her body cool. "She's new in town. I told her I was having lunch here if she had time to drop by." And now that Jaden was planning to return, that was even better. Sheyna didn't have much luck with her own personal life, but at least she got joy out of helping someone else.

She rolled her eyes when she heard Jace's laughter. "You're as bad as Brenna's aunt Nellie with all that matchmaking."

The whole town still raved about how Ms. Nellie

had faked twisting her ankle in order to bring Jabarie and Brenna back together after five long years.

Sheyna tilted her chin high as her eyes traveled across the booth. "I knew Danica would find him irresistible," she returned smartly.

Jace chuckled under his breath. "My brother apparently feels the same way. Look at the two of them. They've forgotten we're here."

He was right. The two only had eyes for each other.

Last month, while at Crazy Nails for her monthly pedicure, Sheyna had taken the chair beside Danica, and, by the time their toes were dry, they were exchanging numbers, and Danica had agreed to participate in her auction.

Watching them, Sheyna couldn't help yearning to have someone look at her that way. "When was the last time you looked at a woman like that?" she dared to ask.

Jace gave the two a quick glance then dropped his eyes back to his plate. "Never."

She swung around on the bench and met his expression. Jace was so stuck on himself that she couldn't resist taunting him just to see if underneath all the steel there was a man who could love and care about one single woman. He tried to act like he was all about business and didn't have time for anything more than a fling, but she just didn't believe that. Somewhere out there was the one woman who would bring the playboy to his knees. And she couldn't wait to see that happen. In the meantime, women beware. Jace Beaumont was just another heartbreaker.

"You're lying. Did you forget about Latonya?" she teased.

Jace gave her a long look while he tried to keep a straight face. Latonya had been his first love. Back then, he was stupid and naive and had allowed his nose to be wide-open over a woman who had been three years older and familiar with running game. "That doesn't count. I was only fourteen at the time and could barely manage to say two words to a girl."

Tipping her head to one side, Sheyna eyed him thoughtfully. "Even back then, talking was the last thing on your mind."

He placed a hand on his chest and smiled. "I beg to differ." As if he suddenly remembered something, one of his eyebrows quirked lazily. "What about Albert?"

Sheyna tried to suppress a giggle. "I was crazy about him, wasn't I? Uh-uh-uh, Albert was the sexiest thing in the seventh grade."

"Yeah, for a boy who picked his nose all the time."

They laughed, and he loved the sound of her throaty laughter.

"That's one thing I like about exploring new relationships, the anticipation. You never know what you're going to experience."

Frowning, Jace reached for his iced tea. "That could be a bad thing."

Sheyna spoke between chews. "Yeah, but it can also be a new and exciting experience. Heart pounding. Palms sweating. Can't sleep at night."

"All the reasons why I don't have time to waste on that kind of foolishness."

She cocked her head toward the two on the other side of the table. "I bet your brother would disagree. A second ago, I swore, I heard him stutter," she said, laughing into his eyes. And shortly after, Jace joined in, as well, as he mocked his brother's starry-eyed expression.

This was the way it had always been between them, laughing and teasing at each other's expense.

Sheyna shifted on the bench, rubbing her hip against his thigh and Jace inhaled slowly, surprised at the impact of her touch. The contact was causing crazy things to happen to him. Ever since he had come out of the restroom and found her sitting in his seat, that funny fluttery feeling had been swimming around in his stomach. He looked at her out of the corner of his eye. The green sweater fitted her curves perfectly. He reached over and picked up half of his corned-beef sandwich to keep from reaching over and touching her.

"Did you get a chance to look at that's candidate's résumé I left on your desk Friday?"

Jace sighed with relief, glad for something, anything,

to distract his attention. Nodding, he finished chewing before responding. "Yep, I got it, but I don't think she's what we're looking for."

"Why not?" she asked.

Her expression was set, her eyes narrowed and glittery, just as they were whenever she was determined to have her way. He felt a wave of disappointment. He enjoyed her more when she was at ease around him, although that was the woman he was unfortunately attracted to.

"Because I think if we're going to hire a training coordinator for the Miami hotel, we need to find someone who can speak Spanish, as well. And that candidate does not."

There was a long silence as she chewed a French fry. By the time she finished, her smile had returned. "Smart thinking. I don't know why I didn't identify that as a necessity."

"That's okay. That's why we work so well as a team."

Sheyna gave him a smile that was meant for only him and Jace felt as if he had been sucker punched right in the gut. Then he made the mistake of looking deep down into those alluring amber eyes and he felt as though he was drowning. She drew him in as no one else had. Sensible, innocent thoughts vanished and were replaced with desire and hunger. In the flicker of a heartbeat, he wanted to kiss her. He craved the taste of her lips, and he felt his body swaying toward her. Seeking just a sample...

The sound of a polite cough, gathered his scrambled thoughts. The others were looking him with amusement, even Sheyna.

He tried to shrug it off. "What?"

Jaden took a sip from his straw. "I said how about the three of us go and catch a movie after this?"

He reached for his drink and took a swallow before glancing at Sheyna. Even though it had been for an instant, before he was interrupted, he had seen the desire in her eyes mirror his. What was going on? "That's up to Sheyna."

She kept her eyes trained on her half-eaten sandwich. "I…uh…no, I'd better pass. I've got a lot of laundry to do. The weekends are never long enough."

He heard the tremor in her voice and knew that she had felt it, too. The attraction brewing between them. The question was what were they going to do about it?

Chapter 4

Sheyna watched the tall curvaceous woman with her hands propped at her slender hips as she sashayed through the rows of tables draped with white linen. The crowd whistled and clapped, and then a man at the back of the room raised the bid to five hundred dollars.

The bachelorette auction was coming along perfectly. Sheyna observed the floor from behind the curtain in the corner of the banquet room while the auctioneer encouraged the crowd of men to raise the stakes. The bidding for bachelorette number ten suddenly became fast and competitive until the auctioneer smacked the gavel on the podium.

"Sold for three thousand dollars to the gentleman at table seven!"

The two hundred guests in the Pearl Room of the Beaumont Hotel cheered and clapped. Her heart danced. They were that much closer to reaching their fifty-thousand-dollar goal for the evening. There were five women left and one beauty in particular was sure to take their pledges way over the top—Danica Dansforth.

"Excuse me, Sheyna?"

Sheyna swung around and faced her assistant, who was clutching a clipboard to her chest, wearing a worried expression. "Valerie, what's wrong?"

She glanced over her shoulder. "Danica is in the lounge and she doesn't look too good."

Alarm came over her face. "Oh, no! She's supposed to go up next."

Valerie pursed her lips then slowly shook her head. "I don't think so."

Hurriedly, Sheyna moved back toward the lounge. Danica was supposed to be the one who brought in top dollar for tonight's fundraiser. If she couldn't go on, Sheyna didn't know what she was going to do.

As soon as she stepped into the room, she found Danica curled up on the couch in a fetal position. When she heard someone move into the room, she raised her head. The twenty-five-year-old redheaded beauty looked so bad Sheyna couldn't help feeling sorry for her.

"Sheyna, I'm so sorry but I feel like I'm coming down with something."

Sheyna moved over to her and placed a hand to her forehead. Sure enough, Danica was burning up with fever. "You need to go home and take something. "Don't worry about the auction. We'll find a replacement."

"Thank you," Danica said with a sigh of relief.

Sheyna moved back out behind the curtain where chatter and nervous laughter filled the air and signaled for one of the other girls to go next while she pondered her next move.

Valerie rushed to her side. "What are we going to do?" she asked quietly, glancing around to make sure no one was listening.

Sheyna heaved a heavy sigh as she watched a petite blonde move out onto the stage. "I guess I'm going to have to fill in."

Valerie's eyes grew wide and round with uneasiness. "Are you sure you want to do that?"

"Doesn't look like I have much of a choice." She moved over to the rack and removed the short, slinky dress Danica was supposed to have worn. She gazed down at the soft light material. Luckily, the two of them both wore a size eight.

"It looks like tonight's event is going to be a success."

The deep male voice cut through her thoughts. Sheyna cringed, then reluctantly turned around. David

Everson was the director of the Sheraton Beach Youth Center and a constant thorn in her side. Sheyna wasn't sure how she had ever thought she loved him.

"I told you I would raise the money," she replied with a defiant tilt of her chin.

David stopped in front of her and allowed his penetrating gaze to linger momentarily on her impassive expression before responding. "Yes, you did, but then you've always been good at everything you do."

She ignored his emphasis on *everything*. The only reason she tolerated him, despite his chauvinist attitude, was that David was a wonderful director, and, regardless of their differences, raising money for the center was something she'd always felt committed to doing.

"Is there something you wanted?" Sheyna asked with a hint of impatience. She had a dress to squeeze into. "Why aren't you out there bidding on any of the women?"

A slight smile curled his lips. "I'm waiting to see this model everyone is talking about."

"She won't be participating tonight."

"What?" His eyes flashed with annoyance. "You guaranteed me you'd raise fifty thousand tonight. I assumed she was your big-ticket item."

There was a pulse beat of silence before Sheyna was able to respond to his childish tantrum. "I will because I'm taking her place. Now, if you'll excuse me."

"You?" David replied, grabbing her arm, halting

Sheyna's quick escape. She watched his eyes grow round before his lips relaxed in a sly smile. "That's even better. At the thought of spending the weekend with you in Las Vegas, I think I'm going to have to bid everything I've got on you."

She jerked her arms away. "Bid on somebody who's interested, I'm not."

"Come on now, we both know you'll do whatever it takes to raise money for the kids," he began as he fingered his neatly barbered mustache. "How about after I win my weekend with you, I match tonight's pledge?"

Sheyna successfully concealed the anger that raced through her body, threatening to explode. Oh, his offer was tempting, but with David there was always a catch. Sorry, she wasn't interested in being on the end of a fishing rod today. "I'm really not in the mood for your games. I need to get ready." Without another word, she hurried off to the dressing room and groaned. She had forgotten about the Las Vegas package deal. As she changed out of her burgundy power suit, she tried to think of another alternative. The last thing she needed was for David to bid on her and win. While reaching for the dress, her mind traveled back to their six-month relationship that had ended so badly. He had been possessive and self-centered. She shuddered at the memories. There was no way in hell she was going to spend an entire weekend with him.

As soon as Sheyna slipped into the dress, she reached for her phone and dialed the corporate office upstairs. If David thought she was going to sit back and allow him to win then he really didn't know her as well as he thought.

Jace boarded the elevator and pushed the button for the first floor. What in the world did Sheyna need that was so urgent he had to stop everything he was doing and come down to the banquet room?

Bachelorette auctions were not his cup of tea. Nothing but a bunch of horny men desperate enough that they had to pay for a date with a beautiful woman. Not that he wasn't above helping a good cause. In fact, the hotel had donated a substantial amount of money to the organization, and had also provided the room and refreshments at no charge.

He heaved an impatient breath. Whatever she needed had to be vital if she'd called him, which was something she rarely ever did. In fact, all week, ever since lunch at Spanky's, Sheyna had been avoiding him and keeping everything between them professional. No chitchat or small talk. No lunches or afternoons on the tennis court. It was enough to drive him insane. Especially since he couldn't stop thinking about her or those hip-hugging jeans.

He climbed off the elevator and moved down the hall. As he drew closer the sounds of men trying to outbid each other perked up his ears.

As soon as he stepped through the double doors, Sheyna's chunky twentysomething assistant raced over to him and grabbed his arm. "There you are! Sheyna's waiting for you." She pulled him behind the stage and pointed to a small room in the corner. "She's in there."

Growing increasingly impatient, Jace strolled over to the room and knocked.

"Come in."

He turned the knob and stepped in then felt the air leave his lungs.

"What took you so long?" Sheyna scolded. "If it were life or death, I'd be dead by now."

He didn't hear a word she said. All he saw was the slinky red dress that hugged every luscious curve of her body. The front dipped low, showcasing the fullness of her breasts. In strappy high heels, she almost reached his six-two height eye to eye.

"What are you doing dressed like that?" he barked, and noticed that he sounded possessive.

She gave him a strange look then shrugged. "Danica got sick at the last minute and I have no choice but to step in."

No wonder he hadn't noticed his brother in the crowd. He'd probably left to take the model home. He stroked a hand across his head and watched as Sheyna leaned over in front of a mirror. Goodness!

Jace swallowed and faked annoyance. "What was so important that you needed me to come down here?"

Her wide eyes tossed him a hint of vulnerability. "I need you to bid on me."

He looked down at her cleavage again. "I don't do auctions and you know it."

Her eyes pleaded with him. "Please, Jace. If you don't, David Everson will, and then I'll be forced to spend the weekend with him in Vegas."

The thought made him clench his fist against his thigh. He remembered that the two had dated briefly and the relationship had ended badly. He never did like the man. "And what do I get if I do?" He didn't really want anything but he loved to see her grovel.

She stepped right in front of him, leaned in close and pressed her breasts against his chest and he couldn't help but feel their softness through the layers of material. His breath caught. Her subtle scent made his heart pound against his chest. She looked so sexy.

"Whatever you want. I'll clean not only your windows but your kitchen floor with a toothbrush if I have to," she replied, then moistened those damn tempting lips and lowered her head a bit.

He let his eyes travel over her bare mahogany skin before traveling up to her face again. Why did she have to look so vulnerable, all soft and needy? The look was totally out of character for Sheyna Simmons. This Sheyna was a girl who was desperate for help. Staring down at her, Jace drew a breath. He would do anything to help her and she should know that. Their friendship meant that much to him.

She didn't pull away when he reached for her. He lifted her chin with his left hand and for a long moment, he simply looked at her. Damn, Sheyna was a beautiful woman. How come he'd just recently noticed that undisputable fact?

In that instant, he knew he would do anything to keep her from spending the weekend with David. "Sure," he murmured, then stroked her cheek with the pad of his thumb. "You've got yourself a deal."

Sheyna watched Jace move out onto the floor and released a sigh of relief. The one man who made her remember she was a woman was the same man who had just agreed to rescue her. She should have known he would have her back. And now she was indebted to him again. It doesn't mean anything, she told herself, but her racing heart thought otherwise.

She moved over to the vanity and took a seat then reached for her blusher. She never was big on makeup, but today a little color was in order. A supermodel she was not, but she would do whatever it took to make the last ten thousand dollars to reach their goal.

"Sheyna, you're on next!" Valerie cried from the other side of door.

She rose, then opened the door and stepped out of the

room. Valerie was standing beside the curtain, signaling for her to hurry up. Her stomach was a tangle of nerves and anticipation. She wanted this experience to be over. She took a deep breath then moved over near the corner and waited for the master of ceremonies to call her name.

"We had a cancellation at the last moment. Danica Dansforth is ill and will not be participating in our auction tonight."

Sheyna heard the disappointment of the crowd and her stomach churned. She was a poor replacement for a model.

"Instead we have the organizer of this function as our next participant in tonight's auction. I introduce Ms. Sheyna Simmons!"

She took a deep breath and stepped out onto the stage.

Jace took a seat at the back of the room then glanced down at his Rolex watch and his mouth thinned with displeasure. He had a thousand things he wanted to do this afternoon and spending time at an auction was not one of them. He couldn't help feeling as if he was at one of those strip clubs he seemed to get dragged to every time one of his friends got married. They were not his cup of tea, either. He preferred his women giving him a private show at home.

He shifted his eyes restlessly around the room, check-

ing the sea of unfamiliar faces, and was relieved when
the MC moved to the microphone and announced that
Sheyna was next. The moment she stepped out onto the
stage, he felt that familiar punch at his abdomen. She
was beautiful. And by the sound of the catcalls and
whistles, he wasn't the only one who'd noticed. Jace
glanced around the room at the hungry expressions on
the men's faces and a strong feeling of possessiveness
took him over. Never had he felt such an overwhelming
need for something as he did Sheyna tonight.

He watched her sashay around the room, showcasing the sleek gown and curvaceous body. He felt himself grow hard with the strong need to possess her.
Where was this coming from?

"We're bidding on a weekend for two in Las Vegas
with accommodations at the Beaumont Grand Chateau.
Can we start the bidding at two thousand dollars?"

"Two thousand dollars!" He heard a man call from
across the room. Jace glanced over and immediately recognized David Everson. Seeing the hungry look in his
eyes Jace knew the man had every intention of having
Sheyna all to himself.

Well, so did he. That competitive streak hit him. And
what Jace wants, Jace almost always gets. "Twenty-five
hundred!" he called with a raise of the hand.

Sheyna looked over at him and winked. Their gazes
connected and he acknowledged that the chemistry he'd

been feeling since she arrived at his town house in that maid's uniform was still brewing between them. Heart pounding. Sizzling. He felt it from on the other side of the room and was thankful he was sitting down. He watched her hips as she moved around another table.

Over the last several months, it had been close to impossible to let go of visions of that sexy uniform and those long legs in stilettos. In that outfit, she had taken his breath away just as she was doing now.

Jace cleared his throat. The thought that she made him feel this way irritated him to no end and he forced himself to remember the only reason why he was here was because Sheyna asked him to, not because he wanted to.

Liar.

He wouldn't have missed this for the world.

"Four thousand," said the gentlemen to his right. Someone to his left then countered and after that the bids kept coming. Jace leaned back in his seat and watched as Sheyna headed over in his direction. Her eyelids were low and her lips slightly parted.

"Ten thousand dollars!"

Sheyna turned and glanced over at David who wore a determined look on his face. She then gazed over at Jace practically pleading for him to counter the offer.

As far as he was concerned, she had nothing to worry about. No way was he going to allow her to spend the weekend with any of the horny bastards in this room.

Especially one bastard in particular. As Sheyna drew closer, Jace knew without a doubt the only person who was going to spend the weekend in Las Vegas with Sheyna was him.

"Fifty thousand dollars!"

There was a collective gasp then a hush settled on the room.

"We have fifty thousand. Do I hear fifty-one? Fifty-one? Going once…going twice…sold to Jace Beaumont for fifty thousand dollars!"

Sheyna's stunned expression finally softened and she mouthed *thank you,* then moved across the room and behind the curtain.

Jace glanced out of the corner of his eye. The look on David's face was priceless. He knew without a doubt there was no way he would have been able to counter his offer. As if on cue, David walked around to where he was standing, bringing the two men face-to-face. Jace gritted his teeth. If he made some offhanded comment, he planned to…

"Congratulations. The center can do a lot with that money. I think if anyone won tonight, it's me. Although Sheyna is beautiful…" David allowed his voice to trail off as he chuckled. "…I don't think a weekend with her is worth fifty thousand dollars."

Jace rubbed his chin thoughtfully, as if considering a response when actually he wanted to break the punk in two. "Then that's where you're wrong. She is worth every penny. If anyone is a winner tonight it is definitely me."

David quickly excused himself and moved across the room. *Arrogant prick, no wonder Sheyna ended their relationship.*

Jace headed toward the stage but swung around when he felt someone tapping him on the shoulder. It was Sheyna's youngest brother, and he didn't look too happy. Darnell Simmons was on his problem list.

"What game are you trying to play?"

Jace frowned at Darnell's question. "What are you talking about?"

"My sister."

Sheyna had two brothers and neither cared much for Jace. "No games, just helping her out."

"Well, she doesn't need your type of help."

"She begs to differ." Jace glanced over at the stage hoping to catch Sheyna in the dress one last time before she took it off.

A muscle flicked at Darnell's jaw. "Listen, Beaumont. Don't get any funny ideas about spending the weekend with my sister at your fancy hotel in Las Vegas."

His traitorous thoughts were already of her squirming beneath him on a bed at his five-star hotel in Vegas. "Listen, Darnell, your sister asked me to rescue her from Everson and I did. So please, give me a break. You've known me long enough to know that she and I are just friends." He had already grown bored with the conversation. He needed to catch Sheyna before she got away.

"I saw the way you were looking at my sister and there was nothing friendly about it. She's my sister and I don't want you to think for a moment she's like those women you're used to having on your arm," Darnell warned.

Jace stepped back and gave Darnell a long hard look. "What are you talking about?"

Darnell's laughter lacked humor. "Don't play dumb, Jace. We all know your track record with women. You're always looking to make the next score. If you're thinking about seducing my baby sister then you need to think again."

When is this ever going to end? They'd been friends since grammar school, and still, her brothers, Darnell and Scott, had always been suspicious of his relationship with Sheyna. It was purely platonic. Or at least it had been. Until recently he would have never thought about being anything other than friends, but now, he wasn't so sure.

Naughty. It was exactly what he was thinking but he had sense enough to keep that thought to himself.

"Darnell, relax. I am not interested in your sister. I'm her boss and her friend. A good friend, might I add, who was able to help her out of a jam." But even as he said that he couldn't get her lush curves or the you-know-you-want-me look she had sent him from across the room out of his mind. He was definitely interested in finding out what that was all about. Jace stepped away from the table. "Besides, this is all about the kids, right?" Without waiting for a response, he turned and followed the seductive scent of Sheyna's perfume behind the curtain. He found her in the little dressing room, struggling with the zipper. A scowl came to her lips when he barged into the room.

"Don't you believe in knocking first?" she scolded.

Every nerve in his body went taut and he quickly returned his eyes to her face. "Good thing I came because it looks like you could use my help." He reached up and released the zipper, and as his fingers brushed her soft skin, blood surged hot and hard to his loins.

The gown began to slip from her shoulders and Sheyna crossed her arms over her midriff to hold it in place as she swung around and frowned. "Why did you have to bid so much?"

"Because it was for a good cause. Besides, you asked for my help."

"But not that much," she pressed furiously.

"Sheyna, a simple thank-you would be nice."

She sighed. "Thank you, Jace. I really appreciate you helping me out this afternoon, but I can never repay you."

"Yes, you can."

He watched as she pondered the possibility while nibbling on her lush bottom lip. "I've got an idea. How about you just take the trip and invite someone else to go with you?"

He shook his head. "Nope. I paid fifty thousand dollars to spend the weekend with you."

She gave him a puzzled look. "Suit yourself, but I must warn you, you're in for a boring weekend."

He had a strong feeling a weekend with Sheyna would be a lot of things, but boring wasn't one of them. "I beg to differ. I think the weekend will be quite interesting."

He knew the exact moment her defensive wall returned. "What if I don't want to go?"

Jace's eyebrows rose slightly. They both knew she was at the disadvantage, and in no financial position to refuse. "Then you can write your own check to the youth center."

"That's blackmail."

His gaze roamed over her face, lower to her mouth and still lower, over her bare shoulders before he leaned closer and softly countered, "Call it whatever you want. Either way we're going to spend next weekend together." He then turned and left the room.

Chapter 5

Sheyna rose and kicked the jack. The last thing in the world she needed was a flat tire. She was exhausted. The event, although quite successful, had drained her both mentally and physically, and she couldn't wait for a hot bath so she could curl up in bed.

She had stayed at the hotel until the last guest had left, then thanked the hospitality staff for all their help and headed out to her car, feeling good that they had exceeded this year's goal. But that moment had passed the second she found herself a mile from home, struggling to jack her tire up. Damn, why hadn't she paid attention when her brother Darnell tried to show her how to use it? Removing the lug nuts would be a cinch. It was using the stupid jack that was the problem. First thing tomorrow, she was going to buy a new jack that would be easier to operate. Unfortunately, that wasn't going to help her tonight. The sun was already beginning to set and in another hour, the road would be pitch-black.

Angrily, she moved around to the driver's side and reached for her purse. She had roadside assistance but in the time it would take to send someone out she could just as easily get one of her brothers to come and assist her instead.

She dialed Darnell's number and when she reached his voice mail, she tried Scott. Seven o'clock on a Saturday night, chances were her brothers were out entertaining the women in their lives.

She hit number three on her save list and glanced up and down the deserted street. At least she was on a well-lit residential road. She started to call her father, but contacted roadside assistance instead. Her father had been complaining of a bad back lately, and even though he would insist on coming to help her, she hated to bother him. He would insist that he was fine but she knew better than that.

The woman on the phone promised to have someone there to help her within the hour. Sheyna contemplated walking home and dealing with her car later but decided she might as well deal with the problem now. The wind whipped and the chill caused her to shiver. She climbed back into the car and closed the door behind her. It would be a while, so she might as well get comfortable.

A gray Tahoe pulled past her then stopped, and as soon as she saw the SUV backing up, she groaned inwardly. *Oh, no! Jace!* He was the last person she wanted to see. The vehicle moved beside her, and the window lowered and she met Jace's concerned look.

"You need some help?" he asked.

She gave him a sheepish grin. "I've got a flat but someone is on their way to help me."

"Then I'll just keep you company until they do." Before she could protest, he backed in behind her and killed the engine. With a groan, Sheyna climbed out and leaned against her car. This could not be happening to her. She was not at all ready to face him. Her face still tingled where he had touched her. She was hoping to have a chance to sort out her feelings before she had to face him at work on Monday.

Jace climbed out and removed his suit jacket and left it on the seat then moved over and examined the jack she had lying on the road beside her flat tire. "You need a better jack."

"Tell me something I don't know. The only person who knows how to work this stupid thing is Darnell."

"I'll get mine." Jace strolled back to his vehicle and used the keyless remote to open the trunk. Within seconds, he returned with a jack of his own.

"You really don't have to do this. Help should be here shortly," she insisted.

"And by the time they arrive, I'll be finished."

"I hate to see you get your suit dirty."

He shrugged as if it was no big deal to get oil on a tailor-made suit. "Sheyna, if I do, I'll take it to the cleaners."

"How about you jack the car up and then I'll change the tire?" When he frowned at her suggestion she added, "The only reason why I hadn't done it was because I couldn't get the stupid jack to work, but nuts are a cinch."

"Would you just relax and let me be a man?"

That was one thing he would never have to worry about. Jace was all man. As he worked, she couldn't help but notice the way the shirt strained across his back and shoulders. How she envied the fabric. Needing to put some distance between her and the man who had her feeling things she'd never wanted to feel for him, Sheyna moved around to the other side of the car, retrieved her phone and called roadside assistance to inform them she no longer needed their help.

While he worked, she stood to the side and watched. Jace didn't look like one to change a tire, let alone break a nail, but in the years they had known each other he had proven himself to be pretty handy. Since she had bought her house, he had come over on several occasions to install light fixtures, an electric garage opener and he had even helped her build bookshelves.

She sighed. This would be the second time in less than four hours that he had rescued her. First the auction, now her tire. She was going to owe him, and knowing Jace the way she did, he was going to expect for her to pay up. The question was, what would he want in return? The thought made her knees weaken and she had to lean against the car for support.

Jace finished tightening down the tire, then put his jack in his trunk. "Make sure you get this doughnut changed tomorrow."

"I'll get it done first thing. Thanks, Jace, for everything."

"Isn't that what friends are for?"

Her breath caught in her chest as she stared up at the man she couldn't seem to get off her mind no matter how hard she tried. "Yeah, I guess it is. You know how I hate depending on a man."

"I know. But do you ever think that maybe a man likes to feel needed sometimes?" He gave her a few seconds to think about his question while he loaded the flat tire and jack into her trunk. As soon as he moved around the car, she looked up, magnetized by his intense gaze.

"I never thought about it before. You like feeling needed?"

He was quiet for a moment before he finally shrugged. "Sometimes."

"Then whenever you need to feel needed, just let me know," she said unsteadily.

He raised one eyebrow in response. "Be careful what you say. I'll hold you to it."

"I already owe you. What's one more thing?" she said with a snort.

His mouth twitched with amusement. "You're right. You do. And I'm ready to cash in."

Her heart began to pound heavily at her chest. "What is it that you want?"

"Dinner."

"Dinner?" she repeated.

"Yep, at my parents' house Thursday night."

Sheyna groaned inwardly. "I've got plans."

"Doing what?"

"Uh…washing my hair."

Reaching up, he raked his fingers through her short, tapered hair. "Your hair looks fabulous. Wash it Friday night instead."

She sighed and crossed her ankles as she leaned back against her car. "Jace, I'd rather make you dinner than spend the evening with your parents." He knew there was no love lost between her and his parents.

"Come on. You owe me."

"Why me?"

He didn't respond for a long moment. "Because if I come without a date my mom is fixing me up with another one of her friend's daughters and I can't stomach her matchmaking while I'm trying to enjoy my dinner."

He looked down for one second then back at her and she saw the desperation in his eyes and couldn't help but chuckle. Jace could be such a baby. Jace knew there wasn't too much she would say no to, but dinner with his parents was taking it a step further than she wanted to go.

Finally, she held up one finger. "The second your mother starts treating me like the little orphan girl, I'm out of there."

"She won't. I promise. In fact, you'll probably be amazed."

"Why?"

He shrugged. "Ever since Jabarie got engaged, my parents have been acting strange."

Her brows shot up. "Strange like how?"

"Very attentive and considerate. Hoping that we'll each marry for love, not money."

She laughed aloud at that. "You're kidding, right?"

The look he gave her said he was dead serious. "No."

Sheyna shook her head in amazement. "This I've got to see for myself."

"So does that mean you'll come?" He gave her a saucy grin.

She let out a little puff of air in defeat. "Yeah, I'll come."

Chapter 6

That night, Sheyna slept better than she thought she would, considering she had a lot on her mind. Sunlight spilled from between her gold curtains, informing her the fog had passed and it was time to wake up. She shifted onto her back then slowly raised her eyelids. The first thought that came to mind was of Jace.

Sheyna groaned and rolled to her side. She had spent the entire night dreaming about Jace so the last thing she wanted was to spend her morning thinking about him. Since it was simply fantasy and nothing more, she allowed her alter ego to succumb to her every desire. Yet the dream had felt so real. His kiss. His touch. Just thinking about it caused desire to swirl at the pit of her stomach. The things he had done to her in her dream, she didn't know if she'd ever be able to look at him the same again.

Frustrated, she sat up on the bed and lowered her legs over the side. Why in the world couldn't she get that man off her mind? Even though it was clear they shared a mutual attraction, they both knew they were all wrong for each other. Being involved with Jace would only bring her unnecessary heartbreak.

Determined to get Jace Beaumont out of her mind once and for all, she rose from the bed, moved into the bathroom and turned on the shower. A long hot shower would be just what the doctor ordered. Then it was off to church for her.

She removed her gown and stepped underneath the hot spray of water and closed her eyes. The second she lowered her eyelids, Jace pushed to the front of her mind again.

How in the world had she let Jace convince her to have dinner at his parents' house? It wouldn't be the first time. She had gone there once for a holiday dinner and his mother had called her "poor child" so many times she had been ready to duct tape the bourgeois woman's mouth. That very day, she had made a solemn vow never to set foot in the woman's house again. Yet, she had allowed Jace to talk her into it.

Sheyna reached for the body wash and squeezed a

dab onto her washcloth. Actually, she should have sent Jace to the lion's den with another one of his mother's fix me ups. That's what he should get for stringing so many women along. But as she lathered her body she knew deep in her heart the rumors weren't true. She had known Jace long enough to know he never set out to hurt any of those women. He just couldn't help it if they chose to fall in love with him only to get their hearts broken in the end.

Quickly she soaped her body while she convinced herself she was too strong a woman ever to fall prey to Jace's charm. Friends, yes. Lovers, never. The only reason she had agreed to dinner was that she owed him for the tire and for the auction, nothing more. On her way home tomorrow, she would just have to stop over at the outlet mall and try to find herself something "suitable" to wear.

As she rinsed off, she thought about the trip ahead and felt her nipples bead beneath the warm water. Together alone in Las Vegas would be the perfect opportunity for him to take advantage of her or for her to satisfy her curiosity.

Enough! She screamed inwardly, then moved to her room to get ready for church service.

After services ended at the Sheraton Beach Baptist Church, Sheyna made the short drive to her father's house. She pulled up onto the long dirt road that led her to the large white farmhouse and parked her car behind her brother Darnell's pickup truck. Scott's Ford Bronco was also in front of the house. From a distance, she could see the two of them blowing leaves away from the house toward the field surrounding the property. Her brothers spent most of their weekends at the farm helping their father maintain the property.

She climbed out of her car and moved up the sidewalk to a wide wooden porch. The front door was open and the screen door unlatched. She stepped into the big old sprawling house and sniffed, then smiled. Meat loaf. Her favorite.

"Daddy, I'm here."

"Come on into the kitchen, precious," he called from the back of the house.

Her heels tapped lightly against the wood floor as she moved down the long hallway past room after room of big solid furniture. She found her father standing at the counter, chopping veggies for a salad.

"Hey, precious." He wiped his hands on a dish towel, then reached for her and planted a kiss on her cheek. "How was church?"

"Reverend Bishop gave a powerful sermon. You should have been there."

"Yes, I hate that I missed it. I wasn't feeling up to going this morning."

She gave her father a worried look. Ever since he'd

been diagnosed with diabetes three years prior, her father's health had become her number-one concern. "What's wrong, Daddy? Sugar high again?"

"No," he began, then hesitated. "I, uh, had a date last night."

"A date?" The idea and the smile on his face took a few moments to digest. "I didn't know you were dating?"

He glanced over his shoulder, eyes twinkling. "Now you do."

She took a seat at the table. "Who's the lucky woman?"

He reached for the cutting board, and carrying it and a red vine tomato over to the table, took a seat across from her. "Jennifer James. She's the new school district administrator."

"Wow!" she said, shaking her head. She had no idea. Her mother had been dead for almost twenty years. During that time she'd rarely ever seen her father go out on a date, and even when she had, he never looked the way he was looking now. It was long overdue.

"I'm happy for you."

He took a deep breath. "I agree. It's been a long time. After your mother, I just couldn't imagine finding someone else. And then Jennifer accidentally backed her Lexus into my car in the supermarket parking lot and we've been seeing each other ever since."

Sheyna raised her elbow onto the table and cupped

her chin in the palm of her hand while she listened. "When do we get to meet this mystery lady?"

"She'll be joining us for dinner this evening."

"Ooh! This sounds serious."

"Maybe. We've been dating for almost three months now." The smile on his face was priceless. He'd struggled to raise three children while grieving over his wife. Never once did Sheyna ever hear her father complain. When her aunt Belle, his older sister, had offered to take his children and raise them herself, he'd refused to break up his family.

If anyone deserved a second chance, it was her father, Shaun Simmons.

While he talked about Jennifer and their common love for science fiction, Sheyna took in his salt-and-pepper hair cut close to his head, his mahogany skin and amber eyes. At fifty-two, her father had aged gracefully.

When he excused himself to get ready for dinner, she smiled after him. Her father was in love. It had been a shame when he'd lost his soul mate to a terminal illness. Now, after almost two decades, he had a second chance. Would she ever find a man to spend the rest of her life with?

Rising, Sheyna moved over to the sink to wash her hands and, while shucking several ears of corn, she thought about her last few relationships. None of those men had even been a potential candidate. She would be thirty on her next birthday and she still had no prospects. She wanted the entire heart-pounding, palms-sweating experience. But no man made her feel that way. Except for Jace.

Gosh, what in the world did a woman do when she found herself lusting over a man who was all wrong for her?

He was a friend and her boss and even if he was willing, which by now she was certain he was, she couldn't see stepping over that fine line. Beside, Jace wasn't anywhere near being ready to settle down. He was young, handsome, with too many women he still needed to see and explore. It was best for her to remember that than to keep thinking about a man she had no business fantasizing about.

However, in her mind she could see him: the cocky quirk to his smile, the gleam in his eyes, the dimples to his cheeks. She could see the two of them walking and holding hands the way lovers do. Shaking her head, she tried to free her mind of the fantasy, but it didn't work for long, by the time she reached for the last ear of corn, thoughts of him had returned. Nothing worked. She couldn't stop thinking about his irresistible smile and dark sable eyes.

The back door opened to her relief, ending any further deliberation.

"Hey, you," her oldest brother, Scott, greeted as he came through the door followed by Darnell.

She smiled at them both as they plopped down at the table, breathing heavily. "You done with the yard?"

"For today," Scott began while propping his leg on the chair across from him. "We'll get back over here next weekend and finish up the far left side."

Darnell leaned back with his arms crossed against his chest. "Dad wants us to stuff a couple of those pumpkin bags so he can decorate the yard for Halloween."

Sheyna carried the pot over to the stove and turned on the burner. She then looked inside the oven and checked on the meat loaf. It was almost ready. "Did either of you know Daddy was dating?"

Her suspicions were confirmed when she noticed them exchange glances.

"Yeah, I happened to show up just a little bit too early this morning and caught her sneaking out, wearing Dad's shirt," Darnell said with a sheepish grin.

She gasped then started giggling. Her father had needs just like anyone else.

Darnell moved over to the sink and reached for the liquid soap then rubbed his hands vigorously under the running water. "What's up with you and that Beaumont cat?"

"What do you mean?"

"Why did he bid fifty thousand dollars on you?"

She kept her head down so the amusement in her eyes wouldn't show. She loved to rattle their chains. Her brothers could be overly protective at times. "He was helping me out."

"Hold up a minute. Jace paid you fifty thousand dollars?" Scott asked incredulously.

"It was for the auction," she explained with a shrug.

Scott laughed and shook his head. "Right."

Darnell was getting angrier by the second. "Scott, you should have seen how he was looking at her." He lifted a curious brow. "So what's the deal? Are you and he going to Vegas together?"

There was silence as her brothers waited impatiently for an answer she took her time giving. "Yes, we're going to Vegas."

"Who's going to Vegas?" her father asked as he stepped into the kitchen in a clean white shirt.

"Sheyna, here, is going to Vegas with her *buddy* Jace."

Her father's eyes traveled from Darnell to her with his brows raised. "Really? Well, I always did like that boy. I didn't know the two of you were dating."

"We're not," she said with a frustrated sigh, then briefly explained the events of the auction, including having to step in to replace Danica at the last minute.

"Well, that was very nice of him. You couldn't go wrong with someone like him in your life."

"Oh, please." Darnell snorted as he sprang from his seat to get a bottle of water from the refrigerator. "We all know him by rep and he's not the kind of man I want my sister dating."

She turned and narrowed her gaze dangerously at her

brother. "Oh, you're just still mad because Lela Riley started dating Jace after she dumped you."

His lips thinned dangerously. "That's not true. We had started going our own separate ways long before that."

"Uh-huh." Sheyna turned to the oak cabinet beside the stove and removed the plates. "It's going to be a minivacation for me."

"Are the two of you sharing a room?"

"Darnell, I don't think that is really any of your business," her father scolded, and Darnell's frown deepened.

Sheyna tried to hide her shock at something she had not even considered: the two of them sharing a room. All she had thought about was the two of them being in the same hotel, but she had forgotten about the suite. But since she had put the prize together she was well aware of the details of the penthouse suite.

Taking a deep breath, she finally replied, "If you must know, we're sharing a suite that has two bedrooms." But, suite or not, the thought of them being alone in one room sent her pulse off the charts.

There was a knock at the door.

"That's probably Jennifer."

She gave her brothers an amused look when their father practically dashed out of the room and down the hall to answer the door.

"What does she look like?" she asked curiously.

Darnell's smile returned. "Oh, you're about to find out now."

Sheyna heard footsteps and then her father stepped into the room followed by a beautiful woman. She sucked in a breath. Jennifer had to be at least half her father's age. She had short dark brown hair that she wore tapered close showing the diamond-studded earrings in her earlobes. She was very petite, and dressed in blue slacks and a conservative baby-blue top.

Shaun cupped her waist then waved his hand toward the group. "Jennifer, I'd like you to meet my children. That's Darnell in the corner who...uh, you met this morning. Scott at the table and this is my daughter, Sheyna."

The woman gave them a warm yet nervous smile. "I'm so glad to finally meet the three of you. Your father has told me so much about you." Her light gray eyes sparkled as she spoke and dimples dominated both cheeks. She could see why her dad was attracted to this lady.

"We're glad to have you here." Her father was smiling so big that she couldn't help but feel happy for him.

"Can I help set the table?" Jennifer offered.

"Sure." Sheyna removed a tablecloth from the drawer and handed it to her. Jennifer moved into the other room to spread it on the table while Sheyna gathered the silverware.

"Dad, she's pretty," Sheyna mentioned when Jennifer had left.

"I think so, too." From the look on his face it didn't matter that she was half his age as long as she made him happy.

"Damn," Sheyna heard Darnell mumble under his breath the second her father left the room.

Laughing, Sheyna commented in a low voice, "Looks like Dad's got more game than you do."

Darnell responded by tossing a carrot at her head.

Chapter 7

Sheyna was a nervous wreck. She had spent the last two hours trying on one outfit after another and barely had enough time left to curl her hair and apply makeup.

Just before she had left for the day, Jace had called down to her office to remind her he would be by to pick her up around six. Sheyna glanced down at the watch on her slender wrist. He would be arriving any minute now and the very thought made her heart beat wildly with anticipation.

Sheyna turned sideways in front of the full-length mirror behind her closet door and smiled, pleased with her choice. The chocolate skirt and cream mock-neck sweater were tasteful and looked quite appropriate with a pair of jungle-print mules. She moved over to her dresser and reached for a small bottle of perfume, then sprayed a sparing amount on her wrists and neck. She didn't know why she had wasted so much time trying to select an outfit. She knew Jace's mother quite well and nothing she could have chosen from her closet would have been appropriate for an evening at Beaumont Manor. The woman had never thought Sheyna was good enough to play kick ball in the park with her son.

Reaching inside her jewelry box, she removed a pair of diamond-studded earrings and put them in her lobes, then decided to wear her matching tennis bracelet. She had a box full of jewelry and most of the pieces she only wore on special occasions. Dinner with Jace's family was definitely one of those occasions.

Sheyna was having a hard time securing the clasp to her wrist when the doorbell rang. Her heart jolted and her pulse pounded. Taking several deep breaths, she reminded herself it was only Jace, then strolled toward the front door and opened it. However, as soon as she saw him her entire body got tense. Their gazes connected and she acknowledged the chemistry was there. She felt it and the intense look in his eyes confirmed that he felt it, as well. Oh, was he a good-looking man who could attract any woman he wanted. But somehow, this evening, he exuded raw, masculine sexuality.

"Hey," she greeted with a smile, then stepped back so Jace could enter her home.

"Hello, to you."

As he moved around her, she took in his appearance. He had changed out of the black business suit he had worn to the office, into a pair of navy-blue Dockers and a two-tone blue sweater. He looked so handsome, she felt heat stir at the pit of her stomach. Her perusal ended when she realized he was staring at her. His eyes raked boldly over her body and then he winked when he caught her eye. In an instant, her skin began to tingle and she resisted the urge to turn and run away.

"Don't you look nice," Jace complimented.

"Thanks, but I need help with this bracelet." She held out her wrist.

"I'm always willing to help a damsel in distress," he teased, then reached for the clasp. As soon as his fingers brushed her wrist, involuntary heat shot through her that she felt all the way to her toes.

Oh, boy. How in the world was she supposed to get through the evening with him making her feel like this?

"There."

Sheyna was glad when he finally released her. Awkwardly, she cleared her throat. "Let me grab my purse and I'll be ready to go." Quickly, she moved back down the hall glad for a few moments alone.

Get it together, Sheyna, a voice whispered in her head.

What was happening to her? It was just Jace, for Pete's sake, but since when did he make her feel like Jell-O inside? She was shocked and mystified by the way she was feeling. Unfortunately, there was nothing she could do about her attraction to him except put on a false front, quick, fast and in a hurry.

She retrieved her purse from the bed, frowned at her reflection in the mirror then made her way back into the living room. Hearing her footsteps, Jace swung around from a picture on the wall he was admiring. The thumb on his right hand was in his pocket and he took a step forward with his lips quirked.

"Ready to go?" he asked.

She drew in a deep breath. "Ready as ever." As she followed him out the door, she could already see that tonight, controlling her emotions was not going to be easy.

Beaumont Manor was a huge two-story brick home on thirteen acres of plush green land overlooking the ocean. A redbrick driveway curved into a semicircle in front of a long porch where family and friends could relax in wicker chairs and enjoy the view of the ocean that ran along the right side of the property.

As he came around to the other side of the car, Jace took another appreciative look and couldn't hold back a grin. He loved the way the skirt hugged her tempting curves and emphasized her long beautiful legs. He dug his hands into his pockets to keep from touching her. Damn, that woman was sexy! He'd never thought in a million years that the tomboy would have grown up to be a turn-on.

"Ready to go in?" he asked.

"Do I have a choice?" she asked with a rueful smile.

"Nope."

"Then I guess I'm ready."

Tossing his head back, he chuckled then slipped an arm across her shoulders. He couldn't help himself. It just felt like the right thing to do.

"They *are* expecting me, right?"

"My mother said to bring a guest. I just didn't bother to tell her who."

She stopped in her tracks and swung around with an incredulous look, his arm slipping from her shoulders. "You're kidding, right? Your mother is going to have a fit when she sees me."

"No, she won't."

A whisper of a sigh escaped her lips. "She hates me."

"No, she doesn't."

Sheyna rolled her eyes heavenward then gave an unladylike snort. "Okay, let me rephrase that…she doesn't think I'm good enough for her son."

"Believe me. She's not going to care," he said as he took her elbow and led her up the stairs to a pair of French doors. "My mother will just be glad I brought a date." He pushed the doorbell.

The door swung open and a husky, dark-skinned man with piercing brown eyes and a generous smile greeted them. "Good evening, Master Beaumont."

"Good evening," Jace said around a groan.

Sheyna had to bite back a smile. Elmer had been with the family for almost twenty-five years, but no matter how many times he was told not to call Jace Master Beaumont, he did it anyway.

"Your family is gathering in the family room."

"Thank you."

Sheyna followed Jace down the long hall. The wooden floors were covered with expensive wool rugs, antique furniture, large green plants and tall vases. Photos adorned the walls. Three chandeliers hung from a ceiling that had to be twenty feet high. They moved past a double staircase. To say the house was beautiful would be an understatement.

As they reached a set of double doors, her steps slowed. She was not looking forward to this at all.

Jace must have sensed her reluctance because he draped an arm across her shoulders again, then smiled down at her and said, "Relax. They don't bite."

Sheyna rubbed a frustrated hand down her face. "That's easy for you to say."

He pushed the door open and they stepped into a

large room. Oak paneling covered any walls that were not occupied by books. Hundreds of books. The decor was gray and burgundy. In one corner was a large brick fireplace and above the mantel hung a professional portrait of the Beaumont family. Straight ahead was a large picture window that looked out onto a private beach behind the house.

As soon as Jace's younger sister, Bianca, realized they had arrived, she sprang from her seat. "Hey, girl! I had no idea you were my brother's date for the evening." She gave her a hug, making Sheyna feel slightly at ease. It was wonderful to have an ally in her corner.

"Mother didn't give me much of a choice," Jace mumbled, then excused himself and moved over to speak to his father.

Bianca took Sheyna's arm and led her over to the bar. "Here, have a glass of wine." She handed Sheyna a long flute then moved in closer and mumbled, "Because you're gonna need it."

Following the direction of Bianca's whiskey-brown eyes, Sheyna glanced around the beautifully decorated room. Sitting on a wingback chair covered in burgundy silk, was a tight-lipped woman and across from her was a prima donna who looked as snooty as she did. They both glared in her direction.

As if she'd read her mind, Bianca mumbled under her

breath, "That's one of my mother's friends, Martha Miller and sitting beside her is her stuck-up daughter, Penelope."

Sheyna stifled her laughter and took a sip from the glass.

"You made it!" Jessica Beaumont exclaimed to her son as she came into the room, looking glorious as usual. Tall and slender, she knew how to make an entrance with the generous sway of her hips in a lavender dress that emphasized her mocha skin. Her long salt-and-pepper hair had been professionally styled so her curls hung loosely around her round face. Her slanted dark brown eyes were large and her cheekbones high.

She moved to her son, and leaning forward, he kissed her cheek. Still standing near the bar, Sheyna knew the exact moment Jessica noticed her because her smile thinned slightly. Taking a deep breath to calm her racing heart, she resisted the urge to latch on to Jace and insist he take her home immediately.

"Well, who do we have here?"

"Mother, you remember Sheyna, don't you?" Bianca offered.

"Of course I do," Jessica said with a tight smile. "You're that poor girl who lost her mother when she was barely ten years old. How are you, dear?"

Sheyna groaned inwardly. *Give it a rest, why don't you?* "Fine, and yourself, Mrs. Beaumont?"

Jessica's face softened and she looked *at* her, instead

of *through* her, for what had to be the first time in all the years she had known her. "Wonderful, thank you for asking."

Jace moved up beside Sheyna and rested a hand lightly at her waist. She was thankful for him coming to her aid, although his warmth was way too comforting. "Dad, you remember Sheyna. She works in my department."

His father gave her a thorough once-over before nodding and beaming. Looking at him gave her a general idea of what Jace would look like when he was older. He was of medium height and weight with dark curly hair graying only at the temples.

Roger Beaumont moved up and gave her hand a firm squeeze. "Of course. I never forget a pretty face. Sheyna, it's so good to see you again. Are you keeping the department in order?"

She was somewhat put at ease by his warm friendly smile. "I'm trying to, Mr. Beaumont."

"Oh, there'll be none of that," he said, then released her hand and gave a dismissive wave. "Call me Roger."

Sheyna smiled weakly. There was no way in hell she would ever call the hand that fed her by his first name. Eyes wide, Sheyna gazed over at Jace then back at his dad. Who was this man and where was the Roger Beaumont who for years had stormed the halls of the Sheraton Beach Beaumont Hotel and barely said two words to her?

A tall white-uniformed man with short hair stepped through the door and announced, "Madame, dinner is served."

"Thank you, Nigel," Jessica said with obvious relief. "Let's all move to the dining room, shall we?"

Penelope and her mother rose and moved toward the door. "Jace, it is good to see you. I was hoping you and Penelope would have a chance to catch up."

"Maybe later." He then made the introductions. Sheyna could tell by the way Penelope's eyes raked her that she thought the woman standing in front of her was beneath contempt. As they talked, Jace pulled Sheyna closer. He smiled, and when she glanced up at him, he raised his brow in a play-along kind of way.

As soon as they were out of the room, Sheyna smacked his arm.

Jace laughed even as he winced in pain. "Hey, what did you do that for?"

She balled her hands angrily at her waist. "Don't try to use me to make your girlfriend jealous."

His eyebrows raised and he shook his head. "She isn't my girlfriend, but she does have her sights set on being my wife," he scowled. "I said to you before you agreed that my mother told me to either bring or date or spend the evening with Penelope."

Sheyna cocked her head. "Oh, so you're using me?" She made an attempt to appear offended, but she was certain her dimples gave her away. She knew Jace well enough to know that he would never intentionally do something like that.

"No, I'm not using you. I just needed help and you were the only person I knew I could count on who wouldn't make more of this than it really is."

"What do you mean?"

"Any other woman would be looking for a relationship but I don't have to worry about that with you."

Their eyes met and in that moment she saw something flicker in his eyes. What? She wasn't sure. Leaning forward, she gazed at his parted lips and thought he was about to press them to hers when he kissed her on the forehead. He pulled back with a smile then grabbed her hand and led her into the dining room. Sheyna swallowed and couldn't understand why she felt disappointed.

The dinner conversation was light chitchat all through the appetizer, lobster bisque, but as soon as the main dish arrived, Martha, who had been watching Sheyna and Jace tickling each other underneath the table, decided to draw attention to Sheyna.

"Sheyna, please tell me, who are your parents?" she asked, sticking her nose in the air and glaring at her with a challenge flashing in her eyes.

Sheyna glanced over at Mrs. Miller's fake smile. She knew exactly what the witch was up to. "Donna and Shaun Simmons."

Martha glanced at her daughter before looking back with a smirk that Sheyna wanted so desperately to slap from her chubby face. "I've never heard of them."

Sheyna was not about to let anyone look down at her just because she wasn't born with a silver spoon in her mouth. Her father had busted his butt and done a wonderful job of raising her and her brothers and she was proud of that.

"My mother died from a brain aneurism when I was ten. My father is a retired school-bus driver. He lives on a three-acre farm right outside the city limits."

"Farm?" she gasped, then looked at her friends with disbelief. "You were raised on a farm?"

Sheyna gave the woman a hard look then replied indignantly, "Yep, and we got pigs and chickens and grow enough veggies that we never have to worry about going hungry."

Out of the corner of her eye, Sheyna saw Bianca bring a hand to her mouth at her intentional use of bad grammar. Jace shifted on his seat and gave a fake cough. Even Roger Beaumont looked tickled by her answer. Mrs. Miller, however, wasn't the least bit amused, instead she looked as if she had been sucking on a piece of sour candy.

"Oh, you poor child." She waited until their server carried in a basket of rolls before continuing. "Penelope just got back from helping starving children in Africa."

Sheyna took one look at Penelope's sunken cheek-bones and wanted to tell her that anorexia was a disease here in the United States. Penelope and her endless legs and her flawless face were not going to get her down.

After that Mrs. Miller started comparing her daughter to Sheyna and it didn't get any better.

"The cook had the night off and I was so hungry I decided to make myself a sandwich and I couldn't even find where we kept the bread," she said with laughter and the others chimed in.

Sheyna bit into a roll and between loud chews replied, "That's nothing. I remember when we were once out of bread and my dad didn't get paid until Friday. I rolled up one hundred pennies and skipped off proudly to the store and came back with a loaf. I made all of us a couple of bologna and mustard sandwiches."

During the entire meal, Mrs. Miller used every chance she had to belittle Sheyna. Bianca brought her napkin to her lips. Out the corner of his eye, Jace saw his father exchange glances with his mother. Even she was mortified. To reassure her, Jace reached under the table and squeezed her hand. Defending Sheyna wasn't an issue because she could hold her own, besides, she wouldn't have wanted his help.

"Ignore them," he whispered when he leaned over for another roll.

She quickly brought her wineglass to her lips. No way

was she just going to let that women make her feel any less than she was, otherwise she would have gotten up from the table and left a long time ago. She rolled her eyes at him for getting her in this mess in the first place.

Afterward, she couldn't wait to escape to the family room where they all had another glass of wine. She immediately brought the clear liquid to her lips, finished it, then reached for another glass. They might as well keep them coming if she was going to survive the night, she thought as she moved over and took a seat on the couch with Bianca.

"I apologize for the Millers' behavior," Bianca murmured. "They can be so stuck up at times. Even Mother was embarrassed."

She did find that surprising. Not that it mattered but deep down it hurt because she could never fit into their world. She glanced over at the corner of the room where Jace was chatting with Penelope. She didn't like the feeling that curdled her stomach as she watched how easily they laughed and carried on. He wasn't flirting, she was certain of that, but Penelope obviously was and that bothered her.

Why?

Oh, she knew the answer. As much as she hated to admit it, she was attracted to Jace and that bugged the hell out of her. She didn't like the feeling one bit.

As soon as Jace moved over to where she was sitting, she signaled that she was ready to go home. He nodded, then she followed him over to his parents to say their goodbyes.

"Thank you for making dinner quite entertaining tonight," Roger said with amusement dancing in his eyes.

Sheyna couldn't help letting a peal of laughter escape her lips as she glanced over at Penelope.

Mrs. Beaumont joined them and squeezed her hand. "I'm so sorry for my friend's behavior this evening. Please join us again," she said kindly.

"You have to admit that the pot roast was good," Jace said as they made their way out to his SUV.

She couldn't do anything but laugh.

They pulled up in front of her house and Jace climbed out of the car and moved around to open the door for her.

"Thanks."

Quiet gratitude shone in his eyes. "No, I should be thanking you for coming with me."

"Hey, that's what friends are for." Friends. That was what she had to keep reminding herself. They were only friends.

They reached her front porch and he took the key from her hand, turned the lock and opened it then handed the keys back to her. His gaze rose to her eyes and Sheyna tried to speak, but her throat was suddenly dry. For the first time since they had been friends, she could not decipher the expression on Jace's face. His sable eyes darkened dangerously and he became completely still, as if he were contemplating his next move.

"I would like one other thing from you," she finally heard him say.

"What's that?"

"This," Jace said as he moved in close.

Sheyna knew trouble came at you like a speeding car—when you least expected it. Unfortunately, she couldn't use that excuse, not with Jace, because she'd known he was no good for her since high school. She had also known that she was attracted to him and the best thing for her to do was to stay far away from him. Though he'd hugged her on many occasions through the years, only in the last six months did his touch, his heat, offer her something else. Something she desperately didn't need. And she had a bad habit of wanting things that she shouldn't have. Jace's kiss was no exception. His moist, warm lips pressed against her own tempted Sheyna in ways she'd only imagined, and for once she gave in to temptation. But with each taste, she tried to convince herself that the kiss meant nothing to her or to him. *Speak for yourself.* His body was saying something entirely different. She was experienced enough to know the hard-on pressed against her stomach meant he was just as aroused as she was.

As he deepened the kiss, Sheyna couldn't resist opening her mouth and inviting him to explore deeper. Jace took the invitation and pulled her tighter into the circle of his arms. As soon as his tongue met hers, she forgot about keeping her guard up, and how badly men could hurt you without even trying; all she could think about was what he was doing to her. And even those thoughts were far from rational.

Jace cradled her head in his hands then dropped light kisses on her mouth and cheek. He made her feel feminine and fragile. She felt young and new to passion, though she'd experienced a man's kisses before. She felt alive in ways she had no business feeling. The walls she'd built carefully to protect her heart began to crumble. And that scared her. She pulled back.

"I don't remember kissing being part of our agreement."

"I don't think a little kiss will hurt. It's my way of showing you how much I appreciate you coming with me tonight." His breath fanned her face and she watched him watching her. This was a mistake and she knew it would never happen again, but right now she didn't want to stop. She wanted to take all she could get because what was happening could never be duplicated.

She closed her eyes and without having to say anything, he pressed his lips to the side of her neck. A moan escaped as his hand ran across her back. Jace rained light, wet kisses along her cheek until he was almost back where she wanted to feel his lips most—her mouth.

Reaching up, Sheyna cupped the back of his head and neck, urging his face toward hers. The warmth radiating from his body surrounded her and then his arms closed around her, pulling her even closer until her breasts brushed against him. The pressure of his chest against her swollen nipples was enough to make her quiver. He was rock solid.

And that isn't the only thing that's hard.

His erection pulsed against her abdomen and should have made her run away, instead it made her pull him closer. Her heart knew what her mind had refused to believe all these months: Jace Beaumont was the one man who could bring life to her big, lonely bed.

His embrace cause a fire to brew within and had her yearning for so much more. The kiss deepened and so did her desire for what only Jace could give her. He nibbled on her bottom lip, sucking gently on her flesh and sending shudders surging through her. A movement in the bushes startled her into standing up straight. She glanced over her shoulder and spotted the neighbor's cat. She released a heavy sigh before turning and looking up at Jace again.

She took several deep breaths trying to calm her

nerves. "I think it's time to call it a night." Feeling un-
kempt, she tried to straighten her dress and hair.

"Good night, Sheyna."

She glanced over her shoulder with a frown. "Just make
sure your mother knows I won't be back next week."

"I'll try to find another date," he replied with a hint
of amusement.

"I'm sure you won't have any problem at all." There
was an uncomfortable silence. Oh, God! What in the
world was she thinking? Things would never be the
same between them again.

"Well…" he said.

He obviously didn't know what to say, either. Get it
back to the way it used to be, she thought. But how?
Her heart thumped, her knees knocked and her mind
was in a frenzy.

"Yes, well…good night," she said, then stepped
inside the door.

"Sheyna, I—"

"I've got a candidate to interview at eight and I haven't
had a chance to finish looking over the résumé," she called
over her shoulder, not bothering to look back. She couldn't
because of what she might see on his face. She'd always
prided herself on her self-control and she had lost it with
him and now she wasn't sure if she'd ever get it back.

"We need to talk about this," he insisted.

Nodding, she said, "Save it for tomorrow."

* * *

Jace stood there long after she had shut the door in his face, realizing how stupid he had been to listen to his little head instead of being guided by the one that rested between his wide shoulders. But want had welled in him so fast, no power on earth could have stopped him from kissing her.

He scowled. He never should have kissed her. And having kissed her, he should have kept it short, but he hadn't expected her to taste so soft and so unbelievably sweet. And then when she'd sighed against his lips he had instantly felt off balance. But now that he was back on his feet, he needed to do a little damage control.

Reaching up, he banged on the door. "Sheyna, open up!" Only a few seconds passed before he heard movement on the other side of the door and the lock turned and opened.

"Yes?" she sighed impatiently.

He gazed down at her, her eyes glazed with passion, lips red and swollen. Damn, she looked sexy, and the need to hold her in his arms again surged through him. What stopped him was the look in her eyes that showed she wished the kiss had never happened. If only he could take back the last ten minutes, he thought.

"I didn't mean for that to happen," he said, and it was true. He'd never intended to kiss her. If anything was to blame, it was his libido. He'd thought he had it under control around her and for the last several months he had been doing an okay job of keeping his distance. But after the chemistry and the strong sexual attraction that had been sizzling between them since she'd cleaned his windows, Jace should have known it was just a matter of time before he couldn't resist temptation, and her luscious lips were too dangerously tempting to ignore any longer.

There was something about Sheyna Simmons that shot straight through him like a glass of brandy straight up. And right now he felt off balance and at a loss for words. He didn't have the slightest idea what to say or how to say it. Damn, when was the last time that had ever happened? He'd never had a problem communicating with women until now. Why now? And why Sheyna? She was no different from the rest of the female population. But even as he finished that thought, he knew it wasn't true.

Sheyna Simmons was in a class all her own.

He could still taste her sweetness on his lips. His arms still burned where he had been holding her. And his erection, well, let's just say, he had a long night ahead.

"Let's just pretend that didn't happen. I'll see you," he finally heard her say, breaking into his thoughts.

How in the world did she expect him to do that? "Wait, we need to talk about what just happened."

Her eyelids fluttered closed. "I'd rather not make more of it than what it was."

"And that's why we need to talk, because it was more. Precious, look at me."

Her eyes narrowed dangerously. "Don't call me that."

He pushed the door open farther so that he could stand before her and clearly read her face as he spoke. "Why, when it's true? You are precious."

The words were out of his mouth before he had a chance to realize what he'd said. The look in her eyes made him wish he could take his words back, but there was no way he could, any more than he could have taken back the kiss. Besides, it was true. He'd heard her brothers calling her precious for years; he used to tease her about the pet name. Now, however, he had to agree, the name was perfect. Sheyna *was* precious. More precious than he'd ever imagined. Why had it taken him so long to realize that?

"Flattery will get you nothing but a fat bottom lip, Mr. Beaumont."

"How about another kiss instead?"

Another frown marred her smooth forehead, and Jace had to bite back the strong urge to just go ahead and kiss her anyway.

"I can't," she said.

"You can't or you won't?"

"Both." She turned. "This is a mistake and we both know it."

Reaching for the door, she brushed his hand. The heat

raced up his arm then settled at his chest. He was still aroused from the kiss and her touching him wasn't helping matters at all. Sheyna pushed him through the door and back onto her porch.

"I'll see you tomorrow," she said, then closed the door behind her.

Jace walked back to his Tahoe feeling a loneliness like he'd never felt. Some way, somehow, he was going to have her in his life, even if it was only temporary.

Chapter 8

There was no way she could go to Vegas next weekend.

For the last couple of days her thoughts had grown stronger and she'd realized she was letting her mind travel in the wrong direction. If Jace suspected in the slightest that she was attracted to him, she'd be setting herself up for heartbreak.

Sheyna shivered in spite of the heat enveloping her. The memory of Jace's kiss hovered heavily in her mind and sent pulses of desire surging through her. In all her years, no man had ever kissed her like that. What was wrong with her? She groaned. She had to be losing her mind because kissing Jace had been insane.

For the last several days she had been avoiding him.

Since Friday she had been coming in early and leaving when he wasn't looking. But it was Tuesday and they always met for coffee and bagels while they had their weekly HR meeting.

She reached for a cinnamon-and-raisin bagel then spread honey-walnut cream cheese on top and took a seat at the end of the table. When she glanced up through the large glass window, she swallowed tightly. Jace was walking toward her at that moment. The tall man with sable eyes and luscious lips. The man who filled her dreams and thoughts. What was going on? They were friends, nothing more, so why wasn't her body listening? Watching him come down the hall, her heart dropped to her stomach then had the nerve to continue pounding.

He was wearing a charcoal-gray suit, tailor-made like all his others, over a crisp burgundy shirt. Without trying to, he stood out with impeccable style and class. Not to mention when he walked, each step hummed with confidence. He was moving down the long hall past the support staff and she felt as if he was her lover coming for her. She pushed the ridiculous thought away. Besides, she wasn't alone. All ten employees that made up the human-resources department were sitting around the table, as well.

As soon as he stepped into the conference room, their eyes met and an arc of heat leaped between them.

She mustered up a smile. "Good morning."

He didn't return her welcoming smile, instead he wore an impatient scowl. "Good morning. Let's get this meeting started."

For the next hour, she tried to listen as he gave the updates on the changes in the employee benefit plan. A day care center was being added to each of the facilities and care would be provided free for the children of all full-time employees as long as they volunteered four hours a week in the center.

The benefits the Beaumont Corporation provided were the best and it was due to Jace's insistence and strong determination to compete with all of the major chains. That was one thing she admired most about him—he was strong willed.

When the benefit manager rose to give a report on the cost, she found herself staring at Jace and didn't hear a word the manager said.

A chuckle reclaimed her attention. She was glad when the meeting was adjourned. Rising, she was headed out the door when she heard Jace call after her.

"Sheyna, stick around a moment. I want to talk to you."

Sheyna braced herself and pretended to play with a hangnail while she tried to think of an excuse to bolt out of the room.

As soon as his secretary exited the room, Jace pulled the door to the conference room shut and swung around.

"Are you avoiding me?" Leave it to him to get straight to the point.

She struggled to keep from trembling. "No," she lied. Jace looked as if he didn't believe her.

"I think you are," he insisted, and leaned his weight across the table. Those firm lips that tormented her thoughts were set in an irritated line.

Sheyna swallowed when she met the determination in his eyes. "Then you need to get your head examined," she replied, pleased that her voice didn't sound as breathless and panicky as she felt.

"How come you've been ignoring all my calls and e-mails?"

Quickly she exhaled and faked nonchalance. "I've been recruiting for the several positions we currently have open. That *is* what you pay me to do."

His intimate study of her face sent tremors through her. "Okay, why didn't you answer my phone call last night?"

"You called?" She knew he had. She'd seen his name pop up on her caller ID and that was exactly why she hadn't answered it. "Because I've been busy."

"Really? New man in your life?" he asked in a tight voice.

Sheyna leaned back against a chair, putting a little distance between them. "That's none of your business."

His deep-set eyes took in her face and inch by inch followed her throat down to the crevice of her breasts, making her heart flutter. After a thoughtful moment, Jace's scowl slowly eased into an unexpected grin. "You're right. It's not any of my business.

Just make sure he understands that next weekend is mine."

She snapped to attention at the possessiveness that registered in his voice. Was he looking forward to spending time alone with her? *Of course he isn't,* she scolded herself. But that did nothing to cool the warmth that radiated through her blood. She gazed over at him and all she could see was his firm mouth and memories of their kiss coursed through her. Reluctantly, she dropped her eyes from those full, succulent lips. There was no way she was going to let him intimidate her.

The sexual attraction sizzling between the two of them was undisputable. Whatever it was about this man that made her body go warm and quivering with wanting him was by no means simple lust. It was more, much more.

Her throat tightened. Was it possible to jump through the fire headfirst without getting burned in the process? She didn't think so. Although, maybe if she finally just gave in to her desire and slept with him and put an end to her longing, this self-torture would be over. She had a feeling that with Jace nothing could be that simple, instead she would be left hungering for more.

Needing something to do with her hands, she

smoothed the front of her beige suit. "I was hoping you'd forget about spending the weekend with me in Vegas."

"No way." He smiled down at her and, like some starry-eyed teenager, her knees all but gave out.

She recognized the gleam in his eyes and the humor that slightly turned his lips. He was challenging her. *Damn him!* She knew even if she kicked and screamed and threatened him with blackmail, he wouldn't back down. *What Jace wants, Jace gets.* He moved over to where she was leaning against the conference table and didn't stop until he was standing directly in front of her. Straightening, she braced herself for a confrontation with him.

The curve of his mouth widened into a flashing grin. "In fact, since we're going to be in the city, why don't we stay an extra day?"

Staring up at the intensity in his eyes, Sheyna swallowed. "Why?"

He looked away long enough to reach for a raisin bagel. "We can go ahead and schedule that sexual-harassment training."

For some weird reason her heart sank. Somehow, she was disappointed to find out it wasn't about her at all. "That's a great idea."

"I'd also like you to interview a few candidates for our housekeeping-supervisor position. The general manager would like a little help," he said between chews.

"But that's your job."

"Yeah, but we need to find someone who has brilliant employee-relations skills, and no one knows that better than you."

He knew flattery would get him everywhere with her. "Sure."

He pulled out his Palm Pilot from his jacket pocket and wrote on the small screen. "Good, then it's settled. I'll have my secretary contact the hotel and arrange the interviews." After putting it away, he smiled. "I knew you wouldn't let me down."

She grimaced as if he'd insulted her. "You think you really know me."

He knew her better than she realized. She was stubborn, very opinionated and always wanted things her way. She was a lot like him.

"I know everything I need to know about you," he admitted as he popped the last of the bagel in his mouth.

"I hate to burst your bubble, but no, you don't," she retorted with a secretive smile.

He reached over and pushed her shoulder with his index finger. "I bet I do. Go ahead, ask me something."

"Okay. What's my favorite color?"

Jace gave a dismissive wave. "That's easy. Green in the winter, and yellow in the summer. Now ask me something hard."

Sheyna leaned back on the table and swung a pen in the air. "How did I get this scar near my lower lip?"

He shook his head. "You and your brother Darnell were racing to the creek and you tripped and fell, hitting a rock and splitting your lip. You needed seven stitches," he said slowly as he reached out and toyed with her hair.

"Leave my hair alone." She looked at him in shock. "How'd you know that?"

That lifted brow said he was amused. "You told me about it ten years ago."

She slapped his hand away and watched the amusement dance in those sable eyes of his. "And you remember?"

He stared into her eyes. "I remember everything about you."

She swallowed, then quickly looked away. "Okay, if that's true then what is it that I want more than anything?"

"Children. Two boys and a girl•just like you and your siblings."

She frowned then reached for another strawberry. That was an easy guess. She'd been talking about having a family since the time they used to play with her Ken and Barbie dolls.

Jace chuckled. "Come on, Sheyna. What else do you think I don't know about you?"

There was a long intense stare before she answered, "What am I afraid of?"

"Getting hurt. You're not as tough as you want everyone to believe." The words were out of his mouth before he had a chance to think about what he had said. And he heard her muttered curse. But it was true. There was a tender, vulnerable side to Sheyna that she kept hidden from even him. She was a woman who was waiting to be unleashed by the right man. He realized he wanted to be the one to discover that side of her.

"You're also ticklish here," he leaned across the space separating them, "and here." Touching her beneath her rib cage was a mistake, heat radiated through him, but it was too late and there was nothing he could have done even if he had wanted to. His amusement swiftly faded as their eyes locked. Suddenly there was nothing between them but an expression of totally unexpected and inappropriate longing shimmering for anyone who walked by to see.

And he couldn't care less.

Her breath caught just as he brought his mouth down on hers and tasted deeply. After a moment of hesitation, during which he was certain Sheyna was going to pull away, she met each stroke of his tongue with equal passion. He dragged her against him. Her arms moved around his neck, and he tilted his head to the right so he had better access to her mouth.

This time he kept his eyes open, waiting for some realization that this was wrong. This was Sheyna and he should be worried he was risking their friendship, especially since he had promised not to kiss her again. But he couldn't think about anything except being right there with her. She belonged in his arms and what he was doing felt so right.

He finally lowered his lids and enjoyed everything that was happening between them. Tongues dancing, hands exploring, bodies pressed as close as possible. A moan escaped her lips and Sheyna gave the way she did everything she was committed to—with everything she had. He pulled her even closer and allowed his hands to stroke her curves.

"I want you," he murmured against her ear, then lowered his lips to her mouth again, but she stiffened and shifted out of his reach. He felt a palm on his chest before she pushed away and stepped around him, putting some distance between them.

"What happened?" he wondered out loud.

Sheyna was quick to respond. "If you don't know then I can't help you."

Somehow everything between them was changing, yet how could he explain to her something he didn't understand himself. The only reason she had ended the kiss was because she had felt it, too. No matter how much she tried to deny it, the attraction was there. The passion, the shared desire. She was attracted to him, as well. She just wasn't prepared to admit it.

Sheyna fascinated him in a way no woman ever had. He couldn't believe now that there was even a time he hadn't known her. They had been friends and coworkers for years, but he hadn't realized what he was missing.

"I'd better get back to work."

He swore under his breath as he watched her exit the conference room, leaving her floral scent behind.

Jace returned to his office and took a seat behind his sprawling walnut desk then glanced over at the stack of candidates résumés that the general manager of the Beaumont Grand Chateau Las Vegas had sent overnight to his office. He had definitely been relieved when Jace had offered to take the burden of refilling the housekeeping-supervisor position off his shoulders.

The last supervisor, Chauncey Atkins, had allegedly been sexually harassing his female housekeeping staff. There had been numerous complaints of behavior unbecoming of a supervisor. Crude jokes, sexist comments and inappropriate touching and petting. He was a lawsuit waiting to happen. Jace rubbed a frustrated hand across his face. Even after several warnings, including threatening disciplinary action, nothing had changed. Instead, Chauncey'd been caught in one of the guest rooms with his pants down. Jace had personally flown down and terminated the prick, who then had had the nerve to question why he was being fired.

The Beaumont Corporation was an equal opportunity employer and was committed to providing and maintaining an exceptional work environment that was free from discrimination and harassment. Anything else was not tolerated. When employees came to work for his hotel, Jace wanted them to be assured that they would be treated fairly and without prejudice. Now he just had to find the right candidate and that was where Sheyna came in.

Lowering his eyelids he could still smell her. Her erotic scent haunted his thoughts and his dreams. It beckoned him to touch and discover the feminine woman she truly had become.

With a scowl, Jace swung around and gazed out his window that overlooked the Atlantic Ocean below. His career had always come first. His job was his love, his life, but today interviewing candidates and training staff were the last things on his mind. All he could think about was Sheyna.

Jace knew that if he hadn't come up with something job related to require their presence in Las Vegas, Sheyna would have backed out of the trip. Now that he had made the trip work-related, they had a better chance of it actually happening.

He felt as if he was losing his mind. All he had done for the last five days was think about that kiss and the young woman who'd returned each stroke with skill and passion. She might have a smart mouth but her lips were soft and supple and he'd dreamed about them since he'd pulled out of her driveway. The hardest thing he'd ever done had been to keep his hands from exploring her lush body.

God, this has been going on for too long.

Six months. They had skirted around their feelings for all that time. Now it was alive and popping between them. The desire was different from anything else. It was about need and want. He rubbed his chin. Something was happening between them. Something undeniable was humming in the air. Sheyna excited his senses and as someone who managed always to stay in control, he didn't like it one bit. He was certain that once he made love to her this attraction that had taken hold of his body would finally disappear.

Breathing softly, he leaned back in the chair and tried to simmer down the physical need he experienced every time he was around her. Yet, it was almost impossible because even as he sat there with his eyelids lowered, he could feel the softness of her lush mouth.

"Excuse me, Jace," his secretary said over the intercom, breaking into his thoughts. "There is a Stephanie Hernandez on line two. She wants to know if the two of you are still on for lunch this afternoon."

He scowled. He had forgotten his lunch with the Wilmington prosecuting attorney. Beautiful but her looks were a blur. With a purring voice, she was a tigress beneath the sheets. He would rather be spending the afternoon with Sheyna. Where was this overwhelming need coming from?

He pushed his thoughts away. Maybe an afternoon with Stephanie was just what the doctor ordered.

"Yes, tell her we're still on."

At lunchtime, Sheyna raced down to the outlet mall for a three-hour shoe sale. Tired but completely satisfied she returned to work with two new pairs of Nine West pumps in her trunk.

She parked her car in the employee parking lot and strolled around to the front of the building in time to watch Jace hop into a red sports car with a beautiful cinnamon beauty behind the wheel.

A lash of unfounded jealousy curled within her. She quickly moved inside the building and across the marble lobby floor to the elevators that took her to the corporate offices that filled the entire seventh floor of the hotel. Breathing heavily, she was shaken by the feeling of jealousy that was too strong to ignore. Why now? Seeing him with another woman had never really bothered her before. As she rode up in the elevator, she tried to convince herself that it didn't bother her to see Jace with yet another one of his bimbos, but despite her best attempts, it did. For some reason she wanted the kisses they'd shared to mean something. She knew that sounded stupid, especially since the last thing in the world she needed was to find herself falling for Jace, but she felt that way just the same. *Especially since I can't get his kisses off my mind.* Last week was bad enough and she was still reeling from the one that morning, which was why she'd decided a quick trip to the shoe store was in order. Nothing took her mind off men better than shoes.

She hung her purse on the back of her door then crossed to the apartment-size refrigerator in the corner and removed a low-fat raspberry yogurt. Reaching into her desk drawer for a plastic spoon, she spotted a brochure in the corner and reached for it.

Beaumont Grand Chateau Las Vegas.

While she ate, Sheyna flipped through the brochure and after looking at the beautiful rooms, she was in awe. The hotel dripped with romance. The stately new hotel had been open barely three months and was booked solid for the next year. But, of course, there were always a couple of rooms reserved for the Beaumont family and friends.

Glancing down at the fine lettering on the front, she remembered being ecstatic when Bianca had donated one of the suites for the auction. She knew that the room plus a weekend with a former runway model would bring in big bucks. She had just never expected to be part of the package.

But as she gazed down at the colorful pages, Sheyna

couldn't help feeling a bit of excitement at finally being able to see the famed Las Vegas Strip while staying in a suite that cost more for a weekend than she made in a month. She was looking forward to shopping and seeing the shows. She wanted to do it all and she would do it with Jace.

Her pulse raced. They were going to share a two-bedroom suite for three nights. Anything could happen. Her heart hammered wildly and she quickly pushed the fantasy aside.

You can do this.

She continued the silent mantra that she'd been chanting for the last several days. She could do this. She could go to Vegas with a man she was sexually attracted to and not fall under his spell. She could enjoy the city, see the sights, enjoy a much-needed break from work, then return home without becoming another notch on Jace's headboard.

But even as she thought that, Sheyna had a strong feeling that it was going to be easier said than done.

Chapter 9

"You're doing *what*?" Brenna exclaimed. Sheyna had just told her about having to fill in for one of the models. Sheyna had also told Brenna about Everson's threat to spend the weekend with her and confided that Jace had stepped in and rescued her.

"Jace and I are going to Vegas next weekend."

Wearing a deep frown, Brenna came around the island in the kitchen and took a seat across from her best friend at the table.

"Do you think that's a good idea?" she asked with a worried look in her eyes.

Sheyna shrugged. "What choice do I have? I owe him for bidding on me."

"No, that was a donation to the community center. That doesn't mean he gets to dictate how you spend your time," she snapped.

"Who says he gets to dictate anything? The prize was a weekend with me in Vegas. I even offered to bail out and let him take someone else, but Jace said he's holding me to my end of the deal."

Brenna leaned back in her chair, her eyebrows raised with concern.

"What's wrong?" Sheyna asked her warily, knowing her friend's knack for honesty.

"Sheyna, you know I love you and I know how crazy you are about Jace."

"I'm not crazy about him!" she quickly denied. "He drives me nuts, just like my brothers."

"Keep denying it to yourself and maybe you'll start believing it, but I won't. The two of you have been dancing around each other for years. Eventually something has got to give."

Sheyna's stomach quivered even as her rational mind took control and offered an explanation. "Believe me, nothing's going to happen between us."

Brenna looked unconvinced. "Why do you keep lying to yourself? You've been in love with him for as long as I've been in love with Jabarie."

Sheyna frowned. Jabarie and Brenna had been crazy about each other since they were thirteen. She and Jace were a different story altogether. "I'm not in love with him. Why in the world would I be in love with someone who acts just like my brothers?"

"Because you love your brothers. They're strong, possessive men who protect those they love. What is so wrong with that?"

"No, they're controlling men who always want things their way," she countered.

"Sounds a lot like you."

"I'm not like that." Sheyna scoffed.

"Yes, you are. You are a very independent and dominant woman and a lot of men feel intimidated by that type of women."

"I think men who do are insecure," she replied with a snort.

"Men are sensitive and have feelings just like women. No one wants to get their heart broken," Brenna said, rising and carrying her glass over to the sink, "which is why I think Jace dates all those airhead women that his mother is always trying to get him to marry. He dates them because he knows he never has to worry about falling in love."

"I think there is another reason why he dates them and that has something to do with their performance in bed," she jested.

"Yeah, but after sex, what's left?"

Amusement curled Sheyna's lips. "More sex."

"Be serious for a moment."

"For what?" Sheyna said, and rose from the chair. "I don't want to talk about me and Jace because there is no 'us.'" She moved over to the refrigerator and reached inside for a bottle of water.

There was a moment of silence before Brenna asked, "How are you planning to handle the weekend in Vegas?"

Sheyna took a long drink and sighed. "Like we handle everything else we do together…as friends." But even as she said that she knew it wasn't the case. Things had changed so much between them. They used to drive up to Philly together and attend basketball games, hang out and go and see movies, but ever since she'd shown up at his house in that damn uniform, things between them had changed. They didn't spend anywhere near as much time together as they used to and they hadn't had a movie night in weeks. Why? The answer was easy. They were both trying to fight their attraction for the other.

"I've loved Jace for almost as long as I've loved my husband, but no matter how I feel about my brother-in-law it doesn't change the fact that he's a dog and I don't want to see you get hurt."

Sheyna waved her hand dismissively. "Oh, puhleeze. The last person I'd ever let hurt me is Jace."

Brenna sighed, knowing when to give up. "I hope so."

"I know so. Now, quit worrying. I learned how to deal

with Jace a long time ago." There was no way she could tell Brenna about the kisses they'd shared because if she did she'd never hear the end of it.

Brenna's eyes were concerned. "I can't help it. You're my best friend and I hate seeing you get your heart broken."

Yep, that was the story of her life. Every time she thought she'd found Mr. Right, he turned out to be Mr. Right Now, and as soon as he'd gotten what he wanted, he was gone. Well, never again. "I have no intention of sleeping with Jace while we're in Vegas. In fact, I plan to ignore him as much as I can. Except while we're working, which, knowing Jace, will be the majority of the time."

She shook her head. "It's a different world in Vegas. The city never sleeps. As soon as you see it work is going to be the furthest thing from either of your minds."

During the summer Brenna and Jabarie had visited the new hotel and she had come back excited about her first visit to Vegas.

"I can't wait to go shopping and take in a few shows while I'm there. I'm going to be so busy, Jace is going to have to find some honey to sit on his lap all weekend."

They laughed.

Sheyna finished helping Brenna address the stack of thank-you cards then headed out to her car. As she moved off the porch Jace's vehicle pulled into the driveway and Jabarie climbed out of the passenger's side.

"Hey, Sheyna. Where's my gorgeous wife?" Jabarie asked, eyes sparkling eagerly.

She pointed to the door and winked. "Inside, waiting for you to get home."

Sheyna waited until he was almost to the door before she moved around the SUV and found Jace studying her, eyes gleaming with appreciation. Her pulse jumped and her throat turned dry. What in the world was wrong with her? She couldn't ignore how handsome he looked and her eyes ate him up. The white baseball cap and matching T-shirt seemed made for him.

"What have you been up to?"

She folded her arms. "Helping Brenna fill out thank-you cards."

There was a slight pause. "You hungry?"

"A little," she admitted.

"Then climb in and let's go get something to eat."

Caught off guard by his offer, her mind whirled as she searched for something to say. Dinner together was definitely a bad idea. "Nah, I've got leftovers at home."

"Save them for tomorrow."

She looked down at her faded jeans and worn T-shirt. Even if she wanted to go out, she wasn't properly dressed for dinner.

His smile broadened. "Come on. I've got a taste for seafood."

He knew exactly how to get her every time.

She moved around to the passenger's side of his SUV and climbed in. As soon as her seat belt was on, he pulled out of the driveway. As she shifted slightly on the seat, her eyes traveled over to him and she couldn't help admiring him in his blue jeans and a button-down shirt. She had known Jace most of her life, and she had seen him in suits, sweats, even shorts, but her favorite outfit on him had always been jeans and a T-shirt. She liked that relaxed, casual look, perhaps because she saw it so rarely. One thing Jace hardly ever did was relax.

"Why are you so quiet?" he finally asked, breaking the silence.

She blushed nervously. "I'm listening to the music."

"Or maybe you're ignoring me."

She wasn't about to admit that his assessment was correct. "Why would I do that?"

"You've been acting strange ever since I bid on you at the auction."

"No, I haven't," she lied.

"Yes, you have, and I want to know why." he insisted.

"It's just strange."

"What's so strange about two friends hanging out for the weekend?" he returned with a grin.

"I guess nothing if you put it that way."

Jace reached over and covered her hand with his. "I promise I won't do anything that you don't want to do."

Why did those words make her feel all funny inside?

"Relax. We've been friends for a long time. Nothing about that is ever going to change," he reassured her.

He was right. She was being ridiculous, making more of it than it really was. When they weren't arguing they always had fun together so why not have fun while in Las Vegas? A smile tipped her lips. As long as he didn't try to kiss her again, she didn't have anything to worry about.

Sheyna stared across the restaurant and spotted Carren, strolling in on the arm of Lawrence Drake, a new dentist in the area. She had seen his face on a billboard every morning as she rode into work.

She tapped Jace lightly on the arm. "Isn't that your girlfriend over there?"

Jace glanced over to his left at the two then returned his attention to her with a shrug. "Ex-girlfriend."

"What happen with you two? Her three weeks up already?" she asked, tongue in cheek.

He took a sip from his water glass before responding. "She wanted a husband and vacation home and I didn't," he admitted. "So she ended the relationship."

"Isn't that the same reason why Jacqueline, Carlita and India ended their relationships with you?"

His lips thinned as if he knew where she was going with this line of questioning. "From day one, I put all my cards on the table and made it clear I wasn't looking for a commitment. I didn't ask them to fall in love and expect more."

She gave him a long hard look. "Nobody sets out to fall in love, Jace. It just happens," she stated.

He shook his head. "Only if you allow yourself to be that vulnerable. I'm not and never will be."

Their waitress arrived and Sheyna waited until she left with their orders before answering. "Jace, you're crazier than I thought. Do you really think you can control your feelings?" She laughed out loud. "I can't wait until the day some woman gets her claws in you."

"Don't hold your breath, because love is one thing I'm not looking for in my life."

Sheyna gave him a dismissive wave. "While you're running away from women, I'm ready to meet Mr. Right and have babies and live in a big white farmhouse."

It was his turn to laugh. "A farmhouse?"

Her eyes narrowed dangerously. "What's wrong with that?"

He took a drink from his glass then smiled. "Actually, nothing. I've always liked your dad's place."

So did she. She adored the starter home she had bought a year ago, but Sheyna hoped someday to afford a home like the one she and her brothers had grown up in. The two-story white house on three acres of land right outside of Sheraton Beach was exactly what she wanted. "Yep, that's my dream."

"Nice dream."

"I think so."

Sheyna excused herself and went into the restroom. As she moved to wash her hands at the sink, the door whooshed open and Carren entered, strolling to the mirror and pretending to fix her hair. Ignoring her, Sheyna turned on the water then reached for the soap dispenser.

"I see you're his new flavor."

"Excuse me?" Sheyna asked, turning from the sink.

A confident smile curled Carren's lips. "If you think things are going to be any different with you, then you're wrong."

Sheyna looked at her reflection in the mirror. She took in Carren's beautiful expensive denim suit and suddenly felt out of place in her jeans.

"We're friends," she finally said.

Following a bitter laugh, Carren turned and faced the mirror and finger combed her hair. "Sure. That's what your mouth says but your eyes tell a different story," she snarled. "He'll keep you around but the second he suspects how you feel, it will be over between the two of you."

Sheyna noticed the pain in Carren's eyes but the bitterness at her mouth kept her from feeling sorry for her. "Jace told me you ended the relationship."

She gave a sad laugh. "That's because he wants to be able to walk away with a clear conscience. So he makes sure you understand a commitment isn't possible and that way you dump him and hope he'll come crawling back to you only to discover he never will." She reached into her handbag.

"Obviously, you've been waiting by the phone."

She dabbed on some lipstick. "Not anymore. I've moved on. Just don't think for a second you're the one woman who can change him because it's not going to happen," she announced bitterly, then strolled out of the bathroom.

Sheyna cursed under her breath. How dare Carren accuse her of being in love with Jace? Just because Carren had been foolish enough to fall in love with him didn't mean she would make the same mistake.

Angrily she soaped her hands and rubbed them vigorously under the running water.

And to think that she had almost felt sorry for her! She could see why they weren't together anymore. Carren was shallow just like all the others had been.

As she reached for a paper towel, Sheyna caught her reflection in the mirror and paused. Was her attraction to Jace that apparent?

Of course not. She chuckled nervously. There was nothing worse than a woman scorned. She tossed the wet paper towel into the trash. She was just jealous, she told herself, but just the same, she'd have to make sure more than ever that Jace never found out how she really felt.

* * *

Sheyna turned the corner only minutes after Jace had seen Carren coming from the same direction. Leaning forward, he watched as she approached the table. Her curvaceous hips swayed with each step. Her breasts jiggled just enough to make him salivate. A frown marred her lovely face.

"Is everything okay?" he asked when she finally lowered herself into the seat across from him.

"Sure, why wouldn't it be?" she said, but he could tell by the stern look in her eyes that something had happened.

"I know Carren said something to you."

She dismissed it with a shrug. "Nothing I can't handle."

"I hope so."

"Don't worry about me," Sheyna said with a significant lifting of her brows. "However, if I were you, I would start sleeping with one eye open."

He scowled. "She's that mad?"

"Worse," she replied with a touch of humor. "Why do you keep doing that?"

He raked a hand across his head then slowly shook his head. "I'm honest, Sheyna. I'm just not looking for a commitment. I'm very forthright about that."

"Then I guess you must be doing something right," she said with a suggestive wag of her eyebrows that sent him into a fit of laughter.

"You are too much."

Their waitress arrived with their food, and Jace sliced into his steak cooked medium well.

"Did Darnell tell you he warned me to stay away from you?" he asked her.

She rolled her eyes heavenward. "Oh, boy! What did you tell him?"

Jace leaned on his elbows and studied her. "I told him that you are a big girl who knows how to handle herself."

She chuckled then her eyes lit up the way he adored. "No wonder he was drilling me at my dad's last weekend. He's never going to let me hear the end of it."

"Is that good or bad?" he asked, waiting for her reaction.

"Oh, that's good. You know my brothers still think they own me."

"You can't blame them for being overly protective. You're a beautiful woman." When she shrugged off his compliment, he added, "Hey, I'm the same way with Bianca."

Dinner was delicious. Their steaks were cooked to perfection. The two spent the meal discussing the one topic that they often agreed on—sports. Both were die-hard Sixers fans. On the ride back to her car, they were both quiet as they rode along the coast. The ocean was raging against the shore. The sun had already begun to set. The windows were down and a cool October breeze drifted into the vehicle. She was trying not to let this feel like a date but it did anyway. The mood was set. All that was missing was Jace walking her to her door and giving her a good-night kiss.

He pulled into Brenna's driveway and killed the engine. The lights were on in the living room, which more than likely meant the newlyweds were curled up on the couch together.

Sheyna took a deep breath and sighed, marking an end to their evening. "Thanks for dinner."

"You're welcome," he replied, then came around and helped her out. He walked her over to where her car was parked in front of the house. As soon as she got behind the wheel, he shut the door behind her. "I'll follow you home," he said as she rolled down her window.

Sheyna shook her head. "You don't have to."

"Yes, I do."

She didn't bother to argue because Jace was a gentleman. He was also stubborn.

Just as he promised, she glanced up into her rearview mirror and watched as he trailed behind her. It was nothing unusual. He had done it many times before. What was different, however, was that when she pulled into her driveway and climbed out of her car, instead of watching her walk to the door, he was coming up the sidewalk.

"Did you forget something?" she asked.

"Yes, I'm afraid I did," he began as he moved up beside her. "And I think you know what it is."

She stared up into his eyes and saw the heat and desire brewing and her body stirred. "No, I'm afraid I don't," she lied. Sheyna knew good and well Jace intended to kiss her. She wanted him to kiss her, wanted more of him than she knew she could possibly ever have. How was it possible for him to make her feel like this with just a single look or touch? But he could. He was making her knees wobble with just the brush of his fingers.

Bending his head, he stepped closer and pulled her into his arms. Sheyna tilted her face up and closed her eyes. As soon as their lips touched, heat ricocheted through her. Rising on her tiptoes, she leaned into his warm embrace. Desire burned through her with each stroke of their tongues. The sensation was powerful. How could something so wrong feel so good? Wanting more, she slipped her arms around his neck and melted against the length of him. Jace deepened the kiss and took complete possession of her mouth. She strained against him, wanting Jace with a desperation that scared her. She wasn't sure how long they stood out on her front porch, necking like a pair of teenagers before Jace finally ended the kiss.

Breathless and with her mind still reeling, Sheyna opened her eyes and stared up at him.

"Give me your keys," he insisted.

Sheyna handed them over then stood back and watched as he opened her door. Next thing she knew

Jace had scooped her up into his strong arms and carried her over to the sofa, taking a seat with her across his lap. She wrapped her arms around him and hugged him tightly as he cradled her in his arms. Why did she feel as if she had waited a lifetime for this moment? Closing her eyes, she snuggled close while his hand slipped beneath her T-shirt. She inhaled as he stroked her belly until the heat of his palm grazed the tops of her breasts. When his fingers slipped beneath the cotton material and touched her breast, she gasped with pleasure. "Jace," she whispered, wanting things she was certain she shouldn't be wanting at all. Yet that did nothing to halt her aching need for his touch. His wet kisses fascinated her. His warm body tempted her. She leaned her head back into the crook of his shoulder, and following his lead, slipped her hand beneath his shirt. He groaned and deepened the kiss.

Within minutes, Jace had swept her T-shirt over her head and tossed it away, then he unclasped her bra and pushed it aside to cup her breasts in his hands. His hands were big and gentle, his fingers driving her wild. His thumb stroked her nipple. Sheyna shook and tried to pretend that nothing mattered beyond these stolen moments. She knew there had to be a stopping point, but she wasn't ready to end what was brewing in her living room, not just yet. For now, she wanted to feel nothing but his hands and the way he brought her body to life.

Jace leaned down and took her nipple in his mouth. His tongue stroked the taut peak, the gentle massage sent waves of desire flooding through her veins and she moaned softly, her fingers caressing his back while her other hand played over the hard planes of his chest.

His hand seared a path down her abdomen and stopped between her legs where he rubbed and caressed. Heat built within her body as he pushed her over the edge. She couldn't control the cry of delight. Oh, but did his hands feel good! He had aroused her and created an intense need, a longing, she hadn't expected.

In minutes Jace had shifted so she was lying on the sofa, chest heaving, body burning with desire as he unfastened her jeans and eased them down, then off onto the carpet. He was watching her expression, holding her immobile with his heated gaze as he brought his hands to her knee and caressed up one leg to the juncture between her thighs. Leaning forward he brought his mouth down hard against hers. Realizing how deeply she wanted him, Sheyna tried to fight for control, knowing at any second they would both be beyond stopping. With stormy reluctance, she pushed against his chest. She wanted this incredibly handsome man with everything she had, but common sense urged caution. She broke off the kiss and untangled herself from his arms.

"I want you," he whispered hoarsely. His jeans

bulged with evidence of his physical need, his voice was filled with emotion.

Her heart thudded when she met his dark gaze. "I want you, too, but there are some things we just can't have in life and this is one of them.

"Let me stay with you tonight," he asked, the tone of his voice demanding yet gentle. Trying to get her body under control, she sat up.

"That would be a mistake." Sheyna wriggled away from him, reached for her T-shirt and lowered it over her head. She didn't even bother putting her bra on, instead she reached for it and pushed it between the cushions of the couch.

Jace rested his elbows on his knees and leaned forward. "Why would making love be a mistake? It seems to me that it's exactly what we both want." His voice was deep and raw.

She preferred not to go there. Unable to come up with a plausible answer, she gave him a look that should have made the answer obvious. But Jace had never been one to accept no as an answer.

"It would be good between us."

She had no doubts about that. She'd heard the stories and knew his reputation. Even now after just a few short minutes, she knew firsthand his ability to arouse a woman.

Sheyna took a deep breath, trying to calm her racing heart. "I don't think so." She slipped her jeans over her hips and fastened them. What in the world was she thinking, allowing him to undress her?

"Scared you might fall in love with me?" he asked with the familiar challenge in his voice.

She tilted her head to study him. "Not as scared as you are of falling in love."

That shut him up. He pressed his lips firmly together and stared over at her and she could feel a wall come up between them. She had seen it before and was starting to wonder if maybe someone in his past had hurt him badly.

"Sheyna," he began. "I know this won't last but why not enjoy the pleasure we find in each other? I'm sure you've had a sexual fling before."

Not with a man who makes me feel like you do. "You've known me long enough to know I don't believe in one-night stands." she answered, and drew a deep breath. "I'm looking for a commitment and I know that is something you could never offer me."

He leaned back on the couch and raked his fingers through his curls. She tucked her shirt inside her jeans and found him watching her. "You're a beautiful woman," he said in a low voice.

"Thank you," she replied, and her heart thumped heavily, then she reminded herself he'd said the same thing to dozens of other women. *Don't get it twisted,* a voice warned. Jace was a player and he made no secret about it.

He grabbed her arm, catching her off guard and

pulled her down onto the couch beside him. The contact sent her heart racing and her body craving for his touch in other areas.

"I can't help being attracted to you, Sheyna," he said by way of an explanation for his actions.

"Do you really want to jeopardize our friendship for a romp in the sack?"

On that note, he released her and heaved a frustrated sigh. He wasn't the only one frustrated that was for sure. "I think it's probably a good idea if you leave."

"Not yet. Why don't we just sit and talk?" he said.

"Sit and talk? About what?" she asked suspiciously.

"What you're looking for in a man," he answered as he shifted on the couch, putting a little distance between them so that she would feel comfortable. What he didn't understand was that as long as he was in the room that was not going to happen.

"You say you want a commitment. What kind of commitment?"

"I want the wining and dining and the proposing down on one knee," she answered, knowing her answer would send him running or he'd immediately back off from trying to seduce her with the fear that she would be foolish enough to fall in love with him. "I want it all, Jace. I want marriage and babies. I want a man who loves me and only me."

"How'll you know when you meet the right person?"

The Playboy's

154

thinking about something, but she di...
They had always shared things in...
to share with her what was bo...
She put her head back ag...
eyes. She was already...
a relationship with h...
terms. Could she...
had to offer...
spun arou...
lose, a...
ris...

"I...
man...
swea...
know...
caus...
and...
her...
time...

how...
bro...
in l...

He looked away, but not before she saw a flash of anger. "Yeah, I've been in love. What about you? And I'm not talking about the kiddy stuff, either."

She curled her legs beneath her and took a few moments to think back. "I thought I was in love several times, but in the end it was so easy to get over them that it couldn't have been love at all. Sometimes I think I'm in love with the idea of being in love, and I look for love in all the wrong places, which is why I've picked up so many losers along the way. But now I want true love, and I'm not settling for anything else, including a no-strings-attached relationship with you."

He was quiet after that and he looked off at the wall behind her. The frown on his face hinted that he was

n't bother to pry.
the past. If he wanted
thering him, he would.
ainst the sofa and closed her
oo attracted to him, but having
m would mean doing things on his
take a chance and accept what little he
thout involving her heart? The questions
d in her mind. Either way, one of them would
d she just didn't think she was strong enough to
not only her heart, but their friendship, as well.

"Sheyna, I loved someone and got my heart crushed," she finally heard him admit. She opened her eyes and listened. "I don't ever want to get hurt like that again."

She realized for the first time that Jace had shared a part of his past that she had known nothing about. It was personal and she knew he was not one to openly share himself with too many people. The fact that he'd chosen to open up to her touched her in more ways than she cared to admit.

"I'm sorry," she replied quietly. "Love sometimes means getting hurt. How serious were the two of you?"

Jace was silent so long she wondered whether her question had intruded too much. He shook his head finally. "I met Julia in my freshman year at Morgan State. I felt exactly like you said you wanted to feel. I couldn't eat. I couldn't sleep."

A muscle worked at his jaw, and his fist was clenched on his knee. While he had chosen to go to Maryland to major in hotel-and-restaurant management, she had stayed close to home and had gone to Wilmington College.

"I practically flunked out my sophomore year trying to keep up with her until my father came down and straightened me out," he ended with a chuckle.

Sheyna gave him a knowing smile.

"She was an English major. Her father worked for the government so she could speak Spanish fluently and had traveled around the world. I proposed during Christmas break and we made plans to wed after graduation." Pausing, he cupped his chin. "Then I started hearing the rumors that she was messing around, but I refused to believe it. Even when she started coming up with excuses why we couldn't spend time together, I refused to believe it. Then one afternoon I happened to spot her walking into a motel not too far from campus. I parked and waited outside the building for four hours until I saw the two of them coming out, hand in hand."

Her chest tightened. She couldn't begin to understand the devastation he must have felt at finding the woman he loved with another man.

"I confronted her that night and Julia admitted she was in love with someone else. After that, I drowned my sorrows in alcohol. She didn't come back for junior year. I heard that she ended up marrying the dude and decided to put school on hold to start a family. That next year, I focused all my energy on my education and then my career and vowed never to let another woman hurt me like that again."

Now she understood his cynical view of love. "Jace, love could be the most beautiful thing. It doesn't always end in heartbreak," she said,

"It makes you too vulnerable," he replied with a scowl.

She placed her hand on his knee. "Yeah, but without it you would spend the rest of your life alone."

"I have my family. I won't ever be lonely."

She actually felt sorry for him. But it also affirmed her decision not to get involved with him because Jace was not willing to risk his heart for anyone. She was no exception. The realization hit her full force. Knowing how stubborn he was, he would control his emotions as he had done in the past, and end the relationship long before those feelings had a chance to blossom. "I guess you know what's best for you."

Jace turned to look at her. He was only inches away now, and she yearned to lean over and kiss him but that was the wrong thing to do if she was trying to make it clear she wasn't interested in him. When she saw the tenderness in his gaze, her heart turned over in response. In the depths of his eyes, desire flashed as hot as a consuming blaze. He closed the distance between them slowly, giving her plenty of time to retreat before he finally kissed her.

Mouths touched, and sent shudders of desire through her body. Jace had opened up to her and shared a part of his past that he'd probably never shared with anyone else and that made their kiss that much more sensational. And desire was building, igniting a hot fiery explosion that melted and shook her. Damn, the man could kiss! His mouth, his tongue were doing things to her. Her calm was shattered with the hunger of his lips.

As much as she wanted to give in freely to the passion, to give to him in return and to do to him even half of what he was doing to her, she couldn't. There was no way she could do that and stand by what she believed in. Sheyna broke away finally, her breath coming in deep ragged gasps. "I think it's time for you to go."

"Are you sure that's what you want?"

"Yes, it is," she said, knowing she was lying. She wanted him so much that it frightened her.

"All right. Good night, Sheyna," he said softly, with a honeyed warmth that stole her resolve. He rose, then pulled her to him. She went willingly into his arms, relishing his hard muscular chest against her softness. Lips pressed, tongues dancing, and the same burning desire and needs flaring. A shiver raced over her. Cupping his neck and holding him, she kissed him passionately for a few minutes before her control returned, and she broke off the kiss.

"Now, go," she said firmly, then watched as he

walked across the room, and she heard the door close behind him. She fell back on the couch, certain that sleep was not going to come easily that night.

Chapter 10

"Jonathan, thank you so much for coming in," she said with the smile that made her applicants immediately feel at ease.

The highly polished young man gave her a warm, enthusiastic smile back. "Thank you. I look forward to hearing from you."

Sheyna shook hands with the candidate, bade him goodbye and, followed by a sigh, headed back to her office.

She had spent most of the morning interviewing chefs for the hotel. Josh Harlan, a chef who had been with the hotel for over fifteen years had decided to move to Boston and open his own restaurant. An executive search was conducted and ads were being run in food magazines and newspapers across America. So far, she had interviewed ten candidates and either they were under qualified or they were demanding thousands of dollars in upgrades to the kitchen as part of their sign-on bonus. Jonathan was the first potentially successful candidate she'd met. He had spent the past three years studying in Paris. She would schedule him to meet with Chef Harlan next week for a more in-depth interview in the restaurant.

As she neared Jace's office, her heart began to beat heavily. She hadn't seen him all morning. Not that she'd been looking. She had been avoiding him. She wasn't ready to face him yet or to bring up what had happened at her house last night.

As she passed his office, she heard him call her name. She slowly retraced her steps and stepped inside his plush corner office. Her mouth suddenly went dry as she gazed across the room at him sitting behind his desk. She rested her hip on the doorjamb and in one fluid motion, he rose and moved around his desk and took a seat on the edge. Her eyes perused the length of him. He looked handsome in a navy blue suit with a white shirt.

"How was the interview?" Jace asked as he crossed his ankles.

She nodded. "I think we've got our first possibility.

Bright, experienced and eager to be part of a team. I'm going to schedule him to meet with Chef Harlan the day after we get back from Vegas."

"Sounds good."

There was a silence and the two just stared across at each other for several uncomfortable moments.

She was the first to speak. "Well, I guess I'd better get back to my office and write my notes while they're still fresh in my head, then I'll be heading out for the night." She glanced over at the clock on the far wall. It was already after five o'clock.

"How about a game of pool this evening?"

Nibbling on the inside of her lip, she took barely five seconds to respond. "I've got things to do."

"Like what?"

She frowned and pressed her lips together for a thoughtful moment. "Like watching a movie."

The look on his face said he didn't believe her. "Scared you're going to lose?"

"Never!" she retorted.

Jace grinned. "Good, then I'll pick you up at seven."

If there was one thing Sheyna was good at, it was pool. Her father had taught her when she was barely five, and on her tenth birthday he had bought a pool table for the recreation room that she and her brothers had been playing on ever since.

So the fact that she hadn't been able to make a straight shot all night had her frustrated. She was up two balls, when she should have beaten her cocky opponent a long time ago.

She was bent over the table, planning her shot when Jace said, "Care to place a bet on it?"

Sheyna scowled then stood upright and frowned at him. "Don't you see I'm trying to concentrate?"

"My bad." He chuckled.

"What do you have in mind?" she asked. He knew there was no way she could resist a challenge.

"If I win I get to kiss you again. If you win, I'll let you off the hook this weekend and let you go to Las Vegas alone."

"Are you serious?" she gasped with disbelief. The audacity of this man!

He nodded his head and grinned. "Have I ever lied to you?"

"Not since sixth grade when you told me Carlos Lennox was waiting for me to ask him to the Sadie Hawkins Dance."

He chuckled, and she joined in at the memory. Jace had known how crazy she had been about Carlos so as soon as she'd spotted him in the hall she had asked him to the dance. Carlos started laughing and told her he already had a date. She'd turned around to find Jace and three of his dumb friends standing next to their lockers laughing at the childish joke. She had spent the evening in her bed crying her eyes out.

"So what's up? Do we have a deal?" he asked, breaking into her reverie.

She watched him with a critical squint. "Why do you have to kiss me?"

"Are you saying you don't like my kisses?"

She wished she could lie but he would see right through it. Nervously, she moistened her dry lips. "I didn't say that."

He lowered his beer bottle and took a step toward her. "Good, then does that mean we have a deal?"

She resisted the urge to step back away from the magnet pulling her toward him. The last thing she wanted him to know was that she was afraid of what she was feeling when she was around him. "I'm not having a fling with you," she said with a defiant tilt of her chin.

Jace held his hands up in surrender. "Hey, I didn't say anything about a fling. All I want is another kiss. I won't do anything that you don't want to do."

That was the problem. Her body yearned to see where those kisses would lead them. Since he had carried her into her house Sunday night all she could think about was having his lips on hers. That was why she didn't need him kissing her.

He gave her a stubborn look. "I guess if you don't lose then you have nothing to worry about."

As long as they were sharing the same air, she had a lot to be afraid of, but there was no way she was going to let him know that.

"Fine, if you win you can have a silly little kiss, and if I win I get to enjoy the suite all by myself." A smile curled her lips. "I think I like the sound of that. Does the room have a Jacuzzi?"

"Yep."

Grinning, she straightened her shoulders. "Then you've definitely got yourself a deal."

"Good." He reached up and cupped her chin with his hand. His eyes were fastened on her mouth as he said, "I can't wait to taste those lips again."

Sheyna stepped away from his touch. The combination of heat from his penetrating eyes, as well as his hand was more than she could bear.

"All right. I believe it's your turn, precious."

She shuddered at the pet name that rolled off his tongue like a gentle caress. "Then get out of my way and give me some space." She leaned over the table and focused on the number-four ball. Jace moved to the other side of the table, but as far as she was concerned it was still too close for comfort. No matter how much she tried to concentrate on the ball, all she could do was watch him out the corner of her eye.

Taking a deep breath, she briefly closed her eyes and set up her shot. It was a pretty easy shot. The ball only needed to be tapped lightly to drop into the corner pocket, which was mere centimeters away. She'd made the same shot several times before and could do it again blindfolded. Taking a breath, she lightly tapped the ball and her shoulders drooped as she barely scraped it. That was not supposed to happen. She heard a chuckle and looked over at Jace with a frown.

"I wouldn't, by chance, be making you nervous?"

"Don't flatter yourself," she retorted, then stepped back from the table.

Jace shrugged and moved to the end of the table and set up his shot. His was an easy one which, of course, he made without hesitation. She wanted to knock that smug look off his face.

She was still beating him by one. She had three balls left on the table. Three to his four. If she got her head on straight, she could win this.

He missed the next one and she breathed a sigh of relief. Her next shot was an easy one. All she had to do was drop it in the corner pocket. She took a deep breath and when it fell into the hole she didn't even try to hide her excitement as she jumped up and down. She was up two again. Unfortunately, the next one she missed.

Jace grinned and set up his shot to hit the nine ball. It wasn't going to be easy. As she stared down at the table a smirk curled on her face. Jace didn't miss a beat.

"You don't think I can make it?"

She held up her hands in surrender. "I didn't say that."

"But you're thinking it."

She managed to shrug and say, "Maybe."

"How about we up the wager?" he shot back.

"What, two kisses instead of one?" she asked, following a quick bark of laughter.

"Nope. I have a little proposition for you to consider."

Heat traveled up her spine. "What kind of proposition?"

"I'll tell you after I win the game," he said, and returned to setting up the shot. "Deal?"

She swallowed. What in the world could he possibly want? Something definitely came to mind but since she was pretty confident she was going to win, she nodded and agreed to his stupid bet.

With the hopes of throwing off his concentration, she moved around the table and stood beside him. He leaned over the table and she was tempted to bump his arm but kept still and held her breath as she watched in disbelief.

The number-seven ball sailed toward the number-five ball and knocked it in the corner pocket then bounced off the side and sank in the side pocket. She couldn't believe it. That shot was impossible. She groaned. This couldn't possibly be happening to her. He had sunk two balls at once. Now they were even. They each had two balls left. Only his next two shots were going to be easy ones. Unfortunately, she couldn't say the same about hers.

She reached for her Corona and took a long swig, needing something to help calm her nerves. For the first time, she considered the possibility that she just might lose.

"You okay?" he asked with an amused look.

"Sure, why wouldn't I be?" she snapped.

He shrugged. "Just asking, considering I'm about to win this game." He bent over the table and set up his shot with a smile.

"You haven't won yet," she mumbled.

"But I'm about to so you might as well get those lips ready."

Her stomach quivered and she found her eyes zeroing in on his thick, succulent lips and part of her was actually looking forward to kissing him again.

She shook off that ridiculous thought and glanced down at the table in time to see a ball sail across the table and land in the right corner pocket. Damn! She had been so distracted that she hadn't even seen him take the shot.

Fuming, she folded her arms against her chest and watched as he set up for his final shot. Please! Please! *Please what?* she wondered. *Please sink it, or please miss?* At this point, she just wasn't sure what she wanted anymore.

She glanced over at Jace in time to see him wink before he pointed with his cue and said, "Side pocket." She felt as though time stood still as he set up the shot and sent the ball sailing into the hole with the eight ball only seconds afterward.

He straightened and her heart began to pound heavily as he removed the stick from her hand and carried them both over to the rack and put them away.

"Would you like another drink?" he asked.

"No," she managed around the lump in her throat.

"Are you ready to go?"

"Yes."

He tilted the bottle and finished his beer then reached for her half-empty bottle and his and carried them over to the counter. He then came back and took Sheyna by the hand and led her from the bar, out toward his Tahoe. As soon as they reached it he leaned her back against the vehicle and lowered his mouth to hers.

The moment his mouth touched hers desire scalded her and left her so dizzy that all she could do was hang on to the strong column of his neck. He pulled her closer into the circle of his arm, her soft curves aligned to his body. When he deepened the kiss, taking possession, she put up no resistance. She couldn't combat her longing. Instead, she returned his kiss, her tongue going into his mouth, and a moan erupted from deep in his throat. Their tongues clashed, and desire, hot and sizzling, drove everything else out of her mind. To her Jace didn't taste of beer, but instead of dark, sinfully sweet chocolate that she craved and had to have her fill of.

He was the king of seduction. Jace Beaumont was a master. He always had been and he always would be. And only the Lord knew why that fact amused and thrilled her, because she didn't. "Why do you do this to me?" she asked, then matched the stroke of his tongue.

"Because I want all of you."

Aroused, he was rock hard and the kiss became more demanding, making her tremble to know that he wanted her so much. The kiss was so beautiful she wanted to cry. A shiver flowed through her body as she took her time savoring what he had to offer. His taste was addictive and she felt herself craving more. She wanted more and was determined to get it.

Jace slipped his hands beneath her jacket, sliding his fingers lightly over her breasts and feeling the hardened buds pushing against the fabric. He freed the top two buttons, slipped his hand inside her blouse and cupped one of her breasts. Sheyna felt a jolt on contact and caught his wrist with one hand and pushed against his chest with the other. She stared up at him and witnessed the undisguised longing in the depths of his eyes.

"I waited all day to do that," he whispered against her damp lips. His gaze lingered on her until she nodded and moved around to her side of the SUV.

They were quiet on the ride to her house. Allowing the sounds of Anthony Hamilton to fill the silence, she took that time to think about how powerful the kiss had been and how she was no longer capable of resisting him.

Walking to her door, Jace covered her hand with his. His skin was warm as she looked up into his eyes.

"Ready to hear my proposition?" he finally asked, breaking the silence.

She swallowed. "Since you won the bet, I don't have much of a choice."

A slow smile touched his lips. He then reached up to run his palm along her cheek. Sheyna tilted her head to the side and studied his intense expression as he spoke.

"While we're in Las Vegas, I want total surrender."

"Surrender?"

"I want you to surrender to me for one weekend. Mind, body and soul."

Her breath shuddered as he continued to gaze down at her while lightly stroking her face. "But, I—"

He pressed a finger to her lips. "This isn't a game. I want you to think about it. I'll be waiting for your answer tomorrow night." He pressed a kiss to her lips.

She watched him leave with her heart pounding rapidly against her chest. Jace was hardheaded and arrogant. Just as he'd always been. So why did she suddenly find those qualities impossible to resist?

Long after he was gone, Sheyna sank beneath her sheets. She felt shattered and intoxicated in equal quantities. Nothing could have prepared her for Jace's proposition. She knew he was attracted to her and wanted a sexual relationship, but no advance warnings could have equipped her for his request for total surrender. She had thought to have fun and have it be all about business while they were in Vegas, and she certainly hadn't expected to be this attracted to him or have that attraction reciprocated.

Surrender for one weekend. Mind, body and soul.

She shifted onto her side while she gave the situation some serious consideration. To have an affair with him would no doubt be an incredible experience, but it would break her own rules, because he had made his intentions clear—there was no future in it. It would be strictly a weekend fling. They would return on Monday and it would be as it was when they had left on Friday.

Sheyna took a deep breath and pressed a hand against her lips, still tasting him there. She might be crazy about his kisses, but she wasn't a fool. She never went further unless she thought there might be a future with a man. But this time would be special, with someone about whom she cared deeply. She would be a fool to turn it down. Yet, if she took what he had proposed that would go against everything she believed in. Giving all of herself to him for one magical weekend—would it be worth it? Her body shuddered in anticipation of what could be. *You won't know unless you try.* Besides, she tried to convince herself, she was only going to be in Las Vegas for an extended weekend. That wouldn't even amount to an affair. It would be, at best, an extended one-night stand. Surely she had more respect for herself than to give in to his request, her desires. Besides, she didn't know if she could separate her heart from the rest of who she was. With a heavy sigh she rolled onto her back and stared up at the ceiling. She was swamped with conflicting emotions. Part of her screamed, "Go for it!" while the other half advised her to run as fast as she could. Common sense said her answer had to be no. She mustn't allow herself more than a few stolen kisses. She knew how dangerous anything more would be if she wasn't careful. But with Jace, her feelings defied the limits of logic. When she was with him she felt an insatiable hunger that she wanted nothing more than to satisfy.

Nope, there was no way she was going to get involved with Jace. She was going to have to keep her head on straight and her feelings toward him under wraps, for she didn't doubt for a moment that he would take advantage of their mutual attraction. What she needed was a distraction. If she was going to have a fling then it needed to be with someone other than Jace. Someone to whom she wasn't physically and emotionally attracted. And she knew just the man for the job.

Chapter 11

Jace cursed under his breath. A night had passed since his proposition and he hadn't seen or heard from Sheyna all day. It was easy to assume she was avoiding him. They worked in the same department at opposite ends of their wing. If she had gone to the bathroom she would've been forced to walk past his office, unless of course, she took the stairs down to the sixth floor. The only reason to do that would be because she was avoiding him.

Unable to stand not seeing her a second longer, he lowered his pen to the file in front of him. He had spent most of the morning reviewing an unemployment claim for a disgruntled former employee.

Pushing the problem aside, Jace strode down the hall

with determination. He was a man on a mission. Sheyna had no idea how much he loved the chemistry between them. He wanted the surge of energy, that delicious heated feeling he experienced that raced through him every time he kissed or touched her. He wanted it and he intended to have it right now.

He strolled around the corner and through a set of double doors then approached a sitting area surrounded by cubicles. He paused when he found Sheyna's door closed, and turned to her efficient fiftysomething secretary, Tina, who was sitting at her desk.

"Where's Sheyna?"

"She's left for the day."

Left? He glanced down at his watch. It was barely three. She hadn't said anything to him about taking the rest of the day off, not that it mattered. She put in more than enough hours each week. "Did she say where she was going?"

Tina smiled sweetly. "She didn't say but I overheard her talking and it seems our dear little Sheyna has a date tonight with the new lawyer in town. He even sent her a beautiful bouquet of roses. They're in there on her desk."

Martin Spires. He'd met him at a political function in the hotel a week ago. The new high-powered attorney had given up New York City to live in a house left to him by his grandparents. He'd decided to hang up his corporate hat and start a practice in their small town. Unfortunately, there was nothing negative Jace could say about the man. He seemed to be a man with a good head who was looking to settle down. Nope, he couldn't say anything negative, except that he was trying to push up on the wrong woman.

Without a word, Jace spun on his heel and headed back to his office. His chest was tight, his temple pulsed. Was it jealousy that he felt? Jace shook his head in denial as he thought it over. Couldn't be, because he didn't do jealous. Besides, he and Sheyna were just friends.

Friends don't kiss each other that way.

Friends weren't supposed to get an erection just from being in the same room. Jace swallowed the knot that rose in his throat. Even now, thinking about holding her in his arms caused a stirring in his pants.

Where the hell were they? He moved behind his desk determined to find out. A couple of phone calls and he wouldn't have any problem finding out where Sheyna and her date were going tonight for dinner.

It was almost ten o'clock when she finally kissed Martin good-night then watched him climb back into his Mercedes. Sheyna closed her eyes and shook her head as he pulled out of her driveway. He was so kind and sweet and almost as boring as his kiss.

"My, my," drawled a familiar, baritone voice, "that

man had his tongue down your throat. What was he try-ing to do, suck out your tonsils?"

"Jace, you're impossible," Sheyna declared as he came up the steps.

He grinned and stopped in front of her, leaning his weight against the iron railing. "I know. My bad."

"How long have you been hiding in the bushes, spy-ing on me?"

"I wasn't hiding," he replied. "Nor was I spying. If you'd bothered to look on the porch as he pulled up in your driveway, you would have seen me sitting in that wicker chair over there. Where, I might add, I've spent the better part of the last hour and a half waiting for you to come home. What did the two of you do, take the scenic route back from Alexander's Steakhouse?"

"No, we did not," Sheyna corrected, enjoying his presence beside her and wishing she didn't. "How do you know where I was, anyway? Don't tell me you've been following me."

"Of course not. I just happened to be in the mood for a steak and spotted the two of you sitting over in the far corner, looking so cozy together."

Seeing the amusement in his eyes, she laughed. "You are impossible. I actually had a wonderful eve-ning with him."

"Quit lying. You were bored stiff."

He'd hit the nail right on the head, but she would rather eat black olives than admit it to him, and she hated olives. "I'm actually seeing him again. I decided if I'm going to have a fling I'd rather it be with someone that I haven't known all my life."

"He's probably just as boring in bed."

"Oh, Jace," she said, and tried hard not to laugh.

He leaned to the side and playfully bumped her shoulder with his. "Come on, Sheyna. Let me show you how good it can be between us."

It was no wonder he'd bedded half the women in Sheraton Beach. He knew just what to say and how to say it. He refused to take no for an answer. He was so charming and so damn appealing, which made it close to impossible to refuse. "Having an affair would be a big mistake, Jace. You know it and I know it."

"But it *is* tempting, isn't it?"

She reached inside her purse for her key and stuck it in the lock. "Good night, Jace. You should be home, packing for Vegas."

"Are you going to tell me what you've decided?"

"About what?"

"You know what. I've been waiting all day for your answer."

With her back to him, she hid a smile. "I didn't know there was a question."

He released a heavy sigh. "No, I gave you a proposition. I want this weekend to mean something. I want it to be special, passionate."

"I thought you didn't believe in passion."

"I believe in passion. What I'm not looking for is love."

At his statement, she swung around and faced him. "So you want me to let you have your way with me for one weekend and as soon as we return home pretend that nothing ever happened between us, right?"

"I didn't mean it like that. Las Vegas is paradise. Let's explore what's been happening between us."

She dropped a hand to her waist. She couldn't remember the last time she had been this badly shaken. "Then you expect me to turn my emotions on and off just like that?"

"Come on, Sheyna, I'm not going to lie, I'm attracted to you in more ways than one. You make me feel things I haven't felt with another woman in a long time and I want to explore those feelings. Tell me something, are you attracted to me?"

Yes. God help her, she was and that was the problem.

She decided the best response was an honest one. Maybe then he would understand where she was coming from. "Jace, you also make me feel things I've never felt before, and I know exploring those feelings means I have to be willing to take a chance, and I'm sorry, you're not worth taking that risk."

"Then who is? Lover boy who just left?"

"No. I don't know who is because maybe I haven't met Mr. Right yet, but when I do it will be about a lot more than sex."

Jace placed his large hand over hers. A shudder raced through her blood. "I feel a lot more than just lust for you."

"That isn't what you said."

"Because I don't want to admit how I feel about you. I'm crazy about you, Sheyna. Hell, you're *driving* me crazy! I want a chance to explore us, but I don't want to ruin things by calling it a commitment or a relationship or anything remotely close to that."

"I'll have to think about it."

"Think about it? Precious, you're driving me crazy!"

"How am I doing that?" she asked with a defiant tilt of her chin.

"I can't eat. I can't sleep. You're affecting my work."

She was flattered. She didn't want to be but she was.

"I want a chance. No pressure. In fact, I'll let you decide when, if at all, but I want you at least to consider it."

She sighed and looked over at him. "You're not going to give up, are you?"

His grin was soft. Not quite victorious, but almost. "Nope."

"Do you intend to worry me to death until I give you an answer?"

His eyes sparkled with mischief. "Actually, I plan to stay glued to your side until you agree to my proposition."

She wouldn't put it past him. "You're ridiculous."

Jace gave a quick shrug. "You can either do it, or you can keep dating people like that, and I can keep popping up when you least expect it."

She had a strong suspicion Jace had made it his business to find out where she was dining this evening. She wouldn't put it past him. Just knowing that and the fact that he had been sitting on her porch waiting for her made it pretty apparent he wasn't making idle threats. He had every intention of wearing her down until she gave the answer he wanted to hear. Damn that man! He could be so stubborn at times.

"Let me let you in on a little secret, precious," he added, as he leaned back against the iron railing, "at some point everyone in this small town is going to notice my persistence, especially since I'm willing to make a public spectacle of myself if I have to. Personally, I don't give a damn about embarrassing myself, so if you…"

Her jaw went slack as she stared up and witnessed the challenge gleaming in his eyes. "That's…"

"Blackmail," he supplied with a firm nod. "Of course it is. I don't want you with Martin Spires. I want you lying naked in my bed." He took her hands and gently brought her flush against him. "Give us a chance to explore what we're both feeling. All I ask is that you come to Vegas with an open mind and consider the possibility of sharing three fabulous nights with me making love to you."

She looked away, fixing her gaze on the pool of light spilling out through the cracked-open door. Of all the men in the world, did she have to yearn for the only one certain to break her heart? "Jace…"

"Sheyna," he said softly, gently, "please, say yes."

She swung away from the circle of his arms and moved across to the end of the porch. The wise thing to do was go into the house and close the door. Or she could simply just tell him no and never to bring up the proposition again. But if she did either of those things, she would spend the rest of her life wondering what might have been. She closed her eyes and swallowed hard. "I always said you were a fabulous salesman. No wonder you're good at your job."

"I only try to sell what I truly believe in and I know this weekend will be one that neither of us will ever forget," he admitted, extending his hands toward her.

Sheyna hesitated, knowing that if she reached for him, if she put her hands in his, she would be agreeing to his proposition but also changing her life forever. And that, as frightening as it was, she was just too drawn to him to flat out say no. Slowly, she lifted her hands and placed them in his. "I'm not promising you anything beyond considering the possibility, Jace."

The warmth and strength of his hands enveloped her, wrapping around her heart and soul. "I'll accept whatever you have to offer and not ask for anything more."

He wouldn't have to ask, Sheyna realized, panic seizing her. All these months, she'd really thought she had the strength to hold him at bay and to keep her feelings under wraps. Good God, she should have known better.

"What time does our plane leave on Friday?" she asked, desperate to get in the house and think about what she had agreed to.

His brow shot up and his smile quirked. "I have us booked on a three o'clock flight."

"All right. I'm taking Thursday off to get ready. I guess I'll see you at the airport on Friday."

He shook his head. "No way. I know you, Sheyna. You're having second thoughts already. If I don't drive us both to the airport, you might not show up. I'll be at your doorstep bright and early Friday morning. We're going to stop for lunch at the beach before our flight. In fact, Thursday, be ready to join me for dinner at my parents. Don't worry, there won't be any women there this time, just you, me and my lovely family," he added with a wide smile.

"B-but…" she stammered.

"No buts, Sheyna. We're going to spend time together, starting tomorrow. So get used to it because I'm not going anywhere."

She was sure he could feel the frantic beat of her heart, could see the apprehension in her eyes. He was so close, Sheyna could see the shadow of new hair on his chin, the fullness of his mouth, his sinfully long, dark lashes. And she could smell the cologne she had bought him for Christmas mixed with the distinctive scent that belonged only to Jace.

His hand rose to her chin. His nostrils flared. She lifted her gaze and looked into his eyes. His eyes slid to her mouth and she sucked in a breath, waiting.

Jace leaned down and pressed his mouth to hers, tasting her the way only he was capable of doing. When his tongue slipped inside her mouth, she purred and felt her nipples tighten beneath her blouse. Her heart missed a beat with every stroke of his tongue and the realization of what was happening between them washed over her, killing the last of the brain cells she needed in order to think straight.

When he finally released her, Sheyna fought to slow her breathing. As she stared up at him, she knew one thing was certain, this was going to be one weekend she would never forget.

Chapter 12

"Why are you smiling?" Sheyna asked, stunned by Brenna's reaction to Jace's proposition. She had waited until Thursday to share her dilemma with her best friend. The two of them sat in Brenna's kitchen, eating cookies she had just taken out of the oven. She had expected Brenna to be livid at Jace's bold attempt at seducing her, instead she seemed quite pleased by the entire idea.

"I'm smiling because I'm starting to think that there might be more to this than I thought." Brenna crossed the mosaic-tiled floor to the small oak table carrying two piping-hot cups of coffee. "Be honest with yourself for a moment. Do you want to spend the weekend with him?"

Sheyna nibbled on a cookie and nodded. "More than I've ever wanted anything else. I don't know why but there is something about Jace, and I feel like, if I don't do this, I'll always wonder 'what if?'"

There was a noticeable moment of silence while they both added sugar to their coffee and stirred before Brenna's head came up, her expression serious. "Are you in love with him?"

"Yes, I am," Sheyna replied around a sigh. "I tried not to be and I know I'm setting myself up for failure by trying to be with him…" Her voice trailed off as realization of what she'd said made her head spin. She gasped for air when she realized she had stopped breathing. How in the world had she fallen in love with Jace Beaumont? It was one thing to love her friend, but somehow she had fallen in love with Jace the man. She felt as if a heavy hand had closed around her heart, squeezing it. How had she fallen for his charm? The cookie stuck in her throat. Damn! Now what?

"I knew you were in love with him!" Brenna squealed with a knowing smile, then raised her mug to her lips and leaned forward. "Go for it. Just be careful." She took a sip. "You know…if you want Jace then you need to show him what he's up against."

Her brow rose. "Are you serious?"

Brenna's hazel eyes sparkled mischievously. "Absolutely, seduce his behind. Show him exactly what he's about to get himself into. Let him know you're nothing like those bubblehead women he's used to dating."

Sheyna took a moment to think about what she was saying and then a slow smile curled her lips as she reached for a warm cookie. "That sounds like a wonderful idea."

"And I want to hear all the details."

A sound caught Sheyna's attention and she turned to find Jabarie standing in the doorway. She could tell by the smirk on his face, he had caught part of their conversation. "Brenna, honey, don't forget we've got dinner at my parents' tonight."

"Sure baby." As soon as he was gone, Brenna rolled her eyes upward. "See what you've got to look forward to when you join the family?" she mumbled sarcastically, then looked to her right to make sure her husband hadn't returned.

Chewing the cookie saved Sheyna from commenting. How she wished, but she knew that, if she decided to sleep with Jace, what they would have would be no more than a weekend fling and there was no reason for her to get her hopes up expecting something else. It was going to be temporary. No matter how much she wished things could be different.

The second the dessert plates were being cleared from the table, Jace told his family good-night and headed straight for Sheyna's house to find out what the hell was going on.

"I made other plans and won't be joining you for dinner."

He had returned home from the office to find her message waiting for him on his answering machine. Determined to change her mind, he had shown up at her house anyway to find that her car wasn't in the driveway. Several calls to her cell phone were ignored.

She told you she wasn't going.

As he drove, trying his best to obey the speed limit, Jace shook his head in disbelief. She had stood him up for dinner. The thought almost made him laugh. She was just as stubborn as he was.

Still chuckling, he turned at the next corner and made the ten-minute drive toward the new subdivision. He shouldn't have been surprised. After all, she had made her feelings clear, and after last week's fiasco, he couldn't blame her. But his pride wouldn't allow him to believe that a woman would rather stay home than spend an evening with him.

Turning at the next corner, he drove down her street and cussed under his breath when he saw her car was still missing from the driveway and the only light on was the porch light that he knew operated on a timer. He took a deep breath while he collected his thoughts. Now was not the time to start jumping to conclusions, but did her cancellation signify that she was turning down his proposal? He hoped not. He wanted her in his arms so badly he could already feel her. He yearned to be inside her body. However, he had already made the decision that if, for some reason, she decided not to accept his proposal, he was going to let her enjoy the weekend in the suite alone. Spending the weekend in Vegas together would be more than he could manage. He didn't think he'd be able to keep his hands off her.

Glancing up into his rearview mirror he caught his reflection and frowned. *Look at you.* He was sitting in front of her house with the engine idling, feeling like a stalker. Where was she? After several seconds, he finally put the car in gear and pulled away. As he drove home, he couldn't help wondering if she was out again with Martin Spires. Jealousy reared its ugly little head again. He couldn't understand why he felt so possessive around her. It was something he hadn't experienced since Julia. And he did not like the feeling, not one bit.

Yesterday he had showed up at the restaurant and had spent his entire meal watching the two of them. Then he had arrived at her house and waited on the porch for them to return.

Jace was starting to think maybe he had pressured Sheyna into doing something that she really didn't want to agree to. He had practically begged her to consider his proposition. Damn, he was pathetic. He hoped she didn't change her mind, but her refusal to have dinner with him and his family suggested otherwise.

He parked in front of his town house then climbed the stairs to the front door. As he turned the key, he saw movement out of the corner of his eye. Quickly, he swung around and his heart did a serenade.

Sheyna.

He just stared and couldn't find the words to ask her what she was doing on his doorstep. The wind was whipping the long trench coat she had tied tightly around her waist.

"What took you so long?" Sheyna asked with that smile he loved so much. "I guess that's what I get for dropping by uninvited."

He glanced past her shoulders and out on the street where her car was parked in front of the house next door. His mind had been so preoccupied, he hadn't even noticed. "I had a stop to make," he said with a nervous chuckle. "Come on in." He opened the door wide, allowing her the room to enter.

She brushed past him filling his nostrils with her sweet floral scent and at the clicking sound on his wood floor he realized she was wearing those black stilettos again. His throat tightened and he began to wonder what she was wearing beneath that coat.

Sheyna dropped her purse onto a small walnut table

in the hall then swung around with a hand planted at her waist. Her coat parted and his eyes traveled up her long lean legs and he swallowed. Oh, boy. Quickly, he brought his eyes back to her face and his breath stalled. There was something in her eyes he'd never seen before. She looked like a woman who was yearning for something that only he could give her.

He resisted the urge to touch her. At least until he found out why she was here. Still, his gaze dropped to her mouth and he remembered how sweet she tasted, and he damn well wanted to kiss her again. Trying to keep his mind off what she was wearing beneath the trench coat was a challenge, especially when he was dying to scoop her off her feet, carry her to his bed and bury himself inside her so deep that one wouldn't know where the other began or ended.

"You got a beer?" she asked, breaking into his thoughts.

"Sure." He took a step toward the kitchen, but she planted a hand on his chest, halting his action.

"Relax, I know where the kitchen is." She then pivoted on her heel and sashayed into the kitchen, with his eyes glued to her behind. As soon as she was out of sight, Jace released a breath he'd had no idea he was holding and raked a frustrated hand across his hair. Why was she here? There was no doubt he was about to find out.

Jace removed his jacket and hung it on the coat tree

beside the door then stepped into the living room. Within seconds Sheyna followed. He stared at her as she moved to the center of the room and popped the tab on the beer, then tilted her head and took a thirsty drink. He watched her slender neck move with every swallow. She finally lowered the can with a big, "Aah! That was good."

The gesture caused his manhood to stir. He finally asked the question that had been burning at his mind. "Why are you here?"

She looked over at him with disappointment. "Jace, if you have to ask, then maybe I need to go home."

"No," he replied quickly. "I'm just surprised, that's all."

Without bothering to answer, she moved over to the sliding-glass door and opened it. Cool, salty air flowed into the room. Taking a deep breath, she tilted her head back.

She wasn't the only one who needed to cool off. He joined her on the balcony.

"So, are you going to tell me why you're here?"

Without turning around, she sighed. "You know why I'm here." She stared off into the night, and he moved up behind her, needing to feel her against him. He closed his eyes as the warmth from her body engulfed him.

"Why are you so quiet?" he whispered close to her ear.

"You."

Jace swallowed. "What about me?"

She swung around, tilted her head and looked up at him. "I've spent the day wondering why, after all these years, am I suddenly so attracted to you?"

He took a step closer. "I've been wondering the same thing."

"And what have you come up with?"

Staring down at her, he shook his head. "I don't know why, all I know is that I can no longer resist you."

She nodded in agreement. "Neither can I."

Reaching up, he lightly caressed her cheek, loving the way her smooth skin felt beneath his fingertips. "And what do you propose we do about it?"

Her lips tipped upward. "Well, I think you've already *proposed* what you'd like to do about it."

"And?" he asked, practically holding his breath as he waited for her answer.

She slid her fingers up and down his arm then locked her hands behind his head and lifted herself up and kissed him gently before deepening the kiss.

"Well?" he asked impatiently against her lips.

After one final kiss, she released him and leaned back just enough so that she could look him in the eyes. "Before I answer, let me make sure I've got this right. You want an uninhibited weekend where I'll surrender mind and body to you and when the weekend is over we'll come back home and it's business as usual." A probing query came into her eyes.

"You make it sound so..."

"So, what? Painful?" she said with light bitterness. "Come on, Jace. It is what it is. You want a relationship without the commitment."

"What's wrong with that?"

Sheyna let out a long, audible breath. "Nothing, as long as I separate my heart from the rest."

"I would never hurt you," he insisted.

"I know you wouldn't...intentionally."

She stepped over to the other side of the balcony and allowed the coat to fall from her shoulders. Jace froze. She was wearing the maid's uniform again. Turning around, her eyes zeroed in on him before she swayed toward him, making him rock hard. She leaned into him, her full breasts pressing against him. The kiss that accompanied this nearness sent his mind swirling.

"Sheyna, I'm serious, I—"

"Shh!" she began with a finger to his lips. "If you haven't noticed, I'm a grown woman," she whispered.

"I've definitely noticed." His hands traveled down her back and settled on her behind.

"I accept your proposition." She didn't give him a chance to respond, instead she kissed him again, and he couldn't fight what he was feeling.

"Are you sure?" he heard himself asking.

"I wouldn't be here if I wasn't. I just hope you know what you're getting yourself into."

Oh, if he hadn't known before he definitely knew now. Sheyna Simmons was a force to be reckoned with.

He swooped down and claimed her lips. They were soft and warm. An ache stirred in his chest then slowly traveled lower to his belly. He groaned in satisfaction as she moved her hands along his back, aligning her body with his. He deepened the kiss and again groaned when her tongue found his.

Sheyna took his hands and raised them to cup her breasts. A blast of heat shot through him. His fingers explored her soft, smooth skin as the kiss continued. She then reached up and lowered one of her straps, leaving her breasts exposed.

"You are so beautiful," he whispered as he fondled her bare breasts in his hand, taking extra time to caress her chocolate nipples. She moaned and leaned against him.

He pinned her against the door and she lifted her leg. He grabbed her, pulling her firmly against him. The warmth of her skin made his blood race through his veins. He slid his hands down her hips and cupped her buttocks. Jace groaned against her mouth while her palms caressed his back then moved to his lower hip. Knowing he couldn't take her was agony.

"We'd better quit," he said, knowing he needed to stop before things got out of control. She nodded in agreement and slowly lowered her leg.

Jace held her against his chest. He wanted her so

badly, but he wanted to wait until the moment was just right. Now that she'd decided she wanted him, he wanted to give her a chance to think it over, and when the time was right, she would have to make the first move. Wrapping his arms around her, he kissed her hair and the side of her neck while his breathing slowed. After this weekend he was certain his life would never be the same again.

Chapter 13

Sleep was the last thing on Sheyna's mind as the limo drove through the razzle-dazzle of Las Vegas Boulevard past neon-lit signs that flashed twenty-four hours a day. She was bubbling with excitement when they finally pulled up in front of the Beaumont Grand Chateau, located at the epicenter of the Las Vegas Strip across from the Winn Hotel. It was beautiful. Sheyna was still reeling from the ride from the airport when Jace stepped past her, opened a door, said, "This is it" and then disappeared inside their suite. Sheyna followed and gasped. Luxurious accommodations, and over two-thousand square feet of living space. The suite was bigger than her entire house. There was an office, two separate bedrooms and a huge plasma TV.

"This room is yours."

The bedrooms were large and spacious and had been specially designed so that they each had a balcony that looked over the Las Vegas Strip. The sight made Sheyna eager to enjoy the excitement below. Glancing around her room she found it was beautiful, feminine and wondrously scented. Sheyna moved across the plush rose carpeting, taking it in, thinking that it had been created for romance. There was a vase of red roses on the dresser, the king-size bed had been turned down, chocolates lay next to the lace-edged pillows. And at the foot of the bed, on the rosy silk-covered bench, sat a huge white box tied with a ribbon.

"It's lovely, Jace," she whispered, slipping her purse from her shoulders. A realization came over her and she laughed softly. "I could stay in this room and never leave."

The mischievous sparkle in his eyes was an admission. "That can be arranged."

She playful punched him in the arm, and he laughed before motioning to the second door in the room. "Through that door is my room. Just so you'll know, I'm leaving it unlocked."

Of course he was. She exhaled and brought the impulse under control.

Jace moved toward her and said softly, "The choice

to join me or invite me into your bed, is yours. I won't force you to make it, Sheyna."

"Thank you," she replied, knowing that he meant it. She crossed to the foot of the bed and fingered the ribbon on the box. "And what's this?"

"A surprise. Go ahead and open it."

Like a child on Christmas morning she eagerly untied the ribbon and removed the lid. Inside she found a red wrap dress. "It's beautiful. You didn't have to do this."

Standing beside the bed with his hands in his trousers pockets, he gave her a soft smile, winked, then said, "Yes, I did. You looked so beautiful in Danica's dress at the auction that I wanted you to have one that color, as well. Besides, I appreciate the fact that you came to Vegas with me willingly."

Desire burned in the depths of his eyes. Good God, he was handsome: tall and broad-shouldered, lips so inviting. She was tempted to cover the space separating them and set about slowly and methodically discarding his T-shirt and jeans. But she knew Jace. If she took a single step toward him, it would be on and popping. She wasn't ready just yet. Goodness, she hoped she could sleep with him and walk away when the time came.

"When did you buy this?" she asked, looking back down at the dress, rubbing the material between her fingers.

"Yesterday afternoon," he answered, eyes dancing

with amusement. He took her hand and guided her to her feet. "I'll let you get settled in," he said, quietly. "How about we go down and have dinner around eight?"

"Okay." That would give her two hours to clear her head and get ready for whatever the evening had to offer. The gleam in his eyes spoke volumes. He was perfectly aware that she'd enjoyed the small intimacy every bit as much as he had. Her heartbeat quickened and her blood warmed.

"You need to know, Jace…" she said softly, unable to draw a breath deep enough to make her voice firmer. "I'm ready to live for the moment but if and when we make love, it's going to be on my terms."

His brow quirked. As did one side of his mouth. Then, slowly, he reached out and took her gently by the shoulders. Bending his head, he stepped closer and she lowered her eyelids.

Jace covered her lips and played around in her mouth with his tongue. She leaned into him, relishing his taste, in the sweet promise of surrendering. He nibbled at her lower lip, catching it gently between his teeth. The sensation was delicious and powerful. Heat raced through her, igniting desire. She slipped her arms around his neck and leaned in closer. Whimpered sounds erupted from deep within her throat, making the desire to make love to him apparent.

Slanting his lips, Jace deepened the kiss while he

wrapped her in his arms and leaned her backward. The kiss was glorious, wild and free. She couldn't breathe, couldn't remain still. Sheyna strained upward, hungering for more, wanting with a need that was so intense it made her tremble.

His breath was rough and uneven against her skin as he moaned her name and then slowly drew his arms from around her, and gently broke the kiss. Breathless, her senses still reeling, Sheyna opened her eyes and gazed up into his.

"Sheyna," he whispered, his breathing ragged, his dark eyes studying her with a look of satisfaction. "I'll see you later." He kissed her once more then stepped back, and gazed down at her. His smile turned mischievous as he winked and softly added, "Enjoy your nap. We've got a long night ahead."

Sheyna watched, stunned, pulse racing as he walked to the door connecting their rooms, opened it and then closed himself away on the other side. Collapsing on top of the soft comforter she stared up at the ceiling, listening to the pounding of her heartbeat and the inner voice of certainty.

Jace was a man to be trusted. He wouldn't force her to open that door and join him in his bed. And as far as she was concerned, he wouldn't have to, because tonight she was going to surrender to him—mind, body and soul. She wanted to make love with every breath and giving in to her emotions didn't matter.

It was crazy. Having an affair with her good friend, her boss, went against everything she believed in. But her heart couldn't bear being denied. Not any longer. She was going to go to Jace's bed willingly and happily. She studied the door that led to his room and smiled. Tonight she planned to fulfill her every dream.

She rolled onto her side and closed her eyes. Right now she needed her rest because tonight was going to be a night the two of them would never forget.

Jace was standing in the living room, waiting for Sheyna. He knew she was up from her nap because he had heard the running water in the private bathroom over an hour ago. While he was getting dressed, he couldn't fight the visions of her naked and wet on the other side of the wall. It took everything he had not to walk through the door separating the two rooms and join her under the spray of water.

He moved over to the floor-to-ceiling window and stared out at the Las Vegas nightlife outside. Signs flashed, cars and people littered the busy streets, hurrying to a show or dinner. But he wasn't thinking about anything but the woman in the other room. He couldn't believe the night had finally arrived. Anticipation caused his heart to thump against his chest.

When he finally heard the doorknob, he turned

around as Sheyna stepped into the room. As soon as he saw her, his chest tightened.

Sheyna was wearing the short red dress that clung to all of her luscious curves and emphasized her small waist and full, round breasts. His gaze lowered slightly and his mouth watered at her long shapely legs. They were the type of legs a man couldn't wait to have wrapped around his waist.

"Sorry I took so long."

He blew out a shaky breath. "You were definitely worth the wait." He took one final look and then a smile tipped his lips.

They took the elevator down to the main floor. People were flooding the casinos, hoping to win big. He guided her through the throng of people. He had been at the hotel numerous times in the last year but he got pleasure out of watching the excitement on Sheyna's face at experiencing the Beaumont Grand Chateau for the first time.

"Look at all these people! Is it always like this?"

He turned to meet her round eyes and nodded. "It will be like this all night long."

He led her down past several specialty shops to Brioni's Restaurant. The establishment was large with numerous tables and chairs packed with a variety of folks and a line of people out front waiting to get in.

"Mr. Beaumont, we are so happy to have you," said the host at the door.

"Hello, Joshua. Sheyna I'd like you to meet the man who keeps things running smoothly at this wonderful restaurant."

"The pleasure is all mine," he replied with a bow.

"Same here."

They entered the restaurant, and delicious smells overwhelmed them. Grilled meats, seafood, pastas and enough desserts to give any kid a tummy ache.

The manager escorted them to a nice table in the corner of the room, which apparently had been reserved for them. It wasn't long before a set of double doors to the kitchen opened, admitting a woman whose face lit up as soon as she spotted Jace. Looking over at him, Sheyna noticed he was just as excited to see her. Jealousy raised its ugly head and she had to fight back the uneasiness in the pit of her stomach. Jace rose from the table, wrapped his arms around the petite little beauty and swung her around in his arms.

"Oh, Jace! I missed you."

When he released her, she turned to Sheyna with a warm smile. "You must be Sheyna."

She looked up at a woman with brown eyes and pouty lips and short curly hair. There was no doubt that she and Jace were related. "I am. Nice to meet you."

"This bighead is my cousin Charlotte."

She swatted him playfully. "I got your big head."

Sheyna rose and before she could offer her hand, Charlotte hugged her instead.

Jace rocked back on his heels. "I can't ever get her to come to the east coast for a visit."

"And look how long it has taken you to come and see us," Charlotte retorted with a playful twist of her lips. "Don't take no mess from this one," she advised Sheyna with a wink. "Enjoy your dinner."

As soon as she moved behind the door, Sheyna leaned across the table with her elbows on the table and smiled. "She seems really nice."

His eyes beamed with pride. "Charlotte's my favorite cousin. Even when we were kids she wanted to be a chef. She traveled and studied abroad for several years and by the time we built the new hotel she was ready to come home, so we offered her the job."

"She seems to love what she does."

"She does. She's spent her entire life in the kitchen. She's got a fat husband to prove it."

With a giggle, Sheyna reached for her menu, loving the delicious aroma that circulated in the room.

"Last month this restaurant was given four stars for the best mouthwatering steaks with a touch of Charlotte's distinctive Creole flair."

"I'm impressed." Sheyna studied the menu a few seconds longer before she knew what she wanted. "I'll have the lamb chops and a baked sweet potato."

Jace lowered his menu and gazed over at her with a look of amusement and decided to have the same. Tonight was starting off with a bang.

After dinner they walked to the other side of the grand hotel, past the theater to Pablo's, a jazz club. As soon as she heard the music, Sheyna started snapping her fingers. "This place has everything."

"This hotel is a world of its own."

They were ushered to the VIP section of the small, dark, crowded club, where they ordered a couple of drinks and took a seat at a small intimate table in the corner.

A half hour passed before Jace lowered his glass and rose. "Let's dance." He reached for her hand and pulled her alongside him.

Her heart skipped a couple of beats as she followed him onto the dance floor. As she had hoped, every woman in the room was looking at him. She took pleasure in knowing he was hers…even if it was just for the weekend.

When he took her into his arms she held on, feeling complete.

"I love holding you," he said next to her ear on the second song.

"I love being in your arms." She inhaled his woodsy scent and her heart fluttered as he pulled her tightly against him. Leaning back, she draped her arms about his neck and stared up at him. For the longest time they stared at each other and she couldn't help thinking about the night ahead. The music slowed down and they were barely moving. Neither was concerned with who or what was going on around them. The look in his eyes was intense and purely sexual. She felt heat settle down between her legs and she knew there was no point in fighting what was happening. She loved him and was willing to take what she could get with Jace. She would deal with the consequences later.

"What are you thinking about?" she asked.

"You don't want to know," he whispered against her ear.

She giggled. "I've got a pretty good idea that it's the same thing that's on my mind."

Dipping his head, he pressed his lips to hers. Oh, yeah, he was definitely thinking about the same thing. What started as a simple kiss changed so suddenly that Sheyna didn't have time to think. All she could comprehend was the need that consumed her as his tongue invaded her mouth.

For the rest of the evening they danced. By the time the clock struck midnight, she was dying to have him inside her. Every nerve in her body was alive and alert and throbbing.

"Let's go," Jace finally said, and escorted her through the hotel and up to their floor. Once outside their suite, he punched in the key code and held the door open for her. Sheyna stepped inside, her heart beating a mile a minute. *This is it.*

"Thanks for a wonderful evening," she replied with her back to the door to her room.

Jace folded his arms across his chest. "I guess this means you're not going to invite me into your room."

A smile curled her lips. "Well, I guess I could. Would you like to go over the presentation for tomorrow?"

"No, I rather do something else," he replied rather frankly.

"Oh." Her brow shot up amusingly.

He reached to caress her cheek. "I told you before we left what I planned to do to you and none of that has changed. If you're ready then you're gonna have to invite me in. Just remember that when you do, I am staying in your bed all night."

Heart pounding, she lifted her chin and looked into Jace's eyes. "Really?"

"Yep."

"Your room or mine?" she rasped.

"Yours."

She grinned then opened the door. He followed her into the room then kicked the door shut. As soon as he did, she stepped into his arms.

She looked up at him then, and his gaze locked with hers. Dark and mysterious, his eyes traveled over her body, making her insides feel like gelatin. The fine hairs on Sheyna's skin rose and her breath hitched. The warmth and scent of him surrounded her. She suddenly became aware of the press of his muscular body against hers. The length of Jace's hardening flesh against her navel indicated he was just as ready as she was. Intense heat radiated from her core.

Friends who became lovers, he'd said, and suddenly the idea didn't sound as crazy as it had before.

Jace kissed her hard and deep then pulled back, just far enough to look into the depths of her amber eyes as he unwrapped her dress and slipped it off her shoulders. It fell to the floor at their feet. Her heart thundered, as he drank in the sight of her standing in front of him wearing nothing but panties and a pair of black heels.

"Damn," he hissed. "You are beautiful, Sheyna."

The look on his face was all she needed. She dragged a breath into her lungs and fumbled at the buttons of his shirt, desperate to be rid of his clothes, aching to feel his bare flesh. She was so nervous she couldn't get the buttons to cooperate.

"Baby, let me do that," Jace insisted, then brushed her hands aside and undertook the task himself. As soon as he was done, she pushed the shirt over his broad shoulders and onto the floor. Staring at his chest, her breathing became ragged. Slowly she rose on her tiptoes and pressed her body against his.

"Sheyna," Jace murmured.

Her breasts brushed his chest and her thighs tangled with his. "I'm right here," she whispered as she raised her hands and slid them over his bare chest then up to his cheeks, holding his face near hers.

He looked down at her and her breath caught. This was it. This was the moment that she had been dreaming about for weeks. Months. She was with the man she loved. And what was about to happen couldn't be more right. "I want you." Her words came out in a rush of warm air.

"Then show me," he whispered as he bent his head toward her lips.

As their lips touched, everything in her shifted. Her wants. Her needs. She gave herself no time to think about what she wanted to do, instead she seized control of the seduction. Her lips grazed the corner of his mouth while she slipped her hands to the front of his trousers, undid the buttons, pushed the fabric aside and took the hardened length of him, in her hands.

Jace threw his head back, sucking a breath through his teeth. Her possession was certain.

He was dying to touch her, certain she was hot and slick with arousal. He knew she would fit him as snugly as her fist was wrapped around him now. He groaned as his erection swelled, and slowly her hand slid all the way up to the tip and back down again. He gritted his teeth against the intensity. If he didn't stop her he was going to finish way too soon. It took every bit of his concentration to grab her wrists and step away from her caress.

Now, with a little distance between them, his vision

cleared enough to recognize the amusement that danced in her eyes. Sheyna knew that she'd rattled his composure to the core and was delighted by it. She was also used to being in control. But not this time, he silently vowed, releasing her hands and setting about stripping away what remained of his clothes.

She watched him, lips parted, eyes sparkling and her breasts rising as her breath caught, falling as she sighed. When he was finally naked, she reached for him again, but he caught her hands and placed them to his hips, saying softly. "My turn to touch."

His tongue boldly claiming her mouth, he slipped his hands down and cupped the perfectly shaped mounds of her bottom before his hands moved from her buttocks, around her hips and down between her thighs. Her eyes widened and a moan escaped her lips as he brushed his fingertips over her damp center. With his other hand he cupped her breast, the thumb teasing her nipple. With both his hands at work, he left a trail of kisses from the corner of her mouth to the tip of her chin and then down the sides of her neck. She made a tiny strangled sound and arched upward, pressing herself against his hands. She gasped, then moaned in a wordless plea for swift deliverance.

"You like that?" he asked.

"Yes, but I would like it better if you got rid of my panties."

He grabbed hold of the waistband and tore them away from her body. "Like that?"

"Yes."

She moaned as he drew her hips firmly against the hardness of his desire, and arched her back as he gently laid her down on the bed.

He wanted to take his time with her, to linger over her, touching and tasting in all the ways the he knew she would like, but he just didn't know how much longer he could hold out for something that he felt he had waited for his whole life.

He left a trail of wet kisses along the length of her throat and downward while she softly released little whimpers. Her eyes were shut, her breathing ragged. Teasing her nipples with his tongue and his masterful fingers, he rewarded her pleas and sent ripples of heat through her body.

His pulse thundered as he skimmed his palms along her inner thighs to brush his fingers over her dampened curls. She shuddered against him when he captured her clit between his thumb and finger, rubbing and feeling her wetness increase. Her fingers were in his hair, holding him close as she cried out in soft puffs of breath.

"Jace," she gasped, drawing his head gently up from her breast. "Please, Jace."

Sheyna moved against him, her hips pressing urgently, and he couldn't deny her, he couldn't deny himself. His hands quickly lifted her hips, drawing her to the very edge of the mattress as he fitted himself between her parted thighs. She moaned and arched up to stroke her heat against the length of his manhood.

Need and desire became one, consuming every part of him. Closing his eyes, he surrendered to the power she had over his mind and body. And then, as though she knew he couldn't bear any more, she slowly eased back and looked up at him, her eyes dark and inviting.

He couldn't deny her, couldn't endure the depth of his wanting any longer. He had never wanted a woman this desperately and the fact that making love to her was no longer a want but now a necessity bothered him, but he would deal with his confusion about his feelings for her later. Right now he had something he couldn't wait another minute to do.

He reached down for a condom from his wallet he had placed on the nightstand, opened the foil wrapper and slipped it on. With his gaze holding hers, he positioned himself between her thighs and pushed forward slowly, deliberately and fully, savoring the warm tightness.

Sheyna gasped and closed her eyes. As soon as he was all the way in he stopped, holding himself still, and gritted his teeth as he fought for control. She tightened about him as he drew back, whimpered when he filled her again. Her legs wrapped around him, he moved rhythmically in and out again and again. Sheyna arched up to meet him, the unbearable need deepening and intensifying with every beat of his heart. He pressed against her, rubbing the base against her clit. She gasped and came up off the bed. He pumped harder, forcing her back down onto the mattress. The rhythm of their dance quickened, hardened as they rode the growing waves of ecstasy.

He drew a sharp breath at the intensity. She lifted her hips to meet every stroke and he pounded into her until he finally surrendered to the irresistible wave. After he felt her contract around him, followed by her cries of completion, with a triumphant moan he spilled inside her.

Jace slowly returned to earth, feeling incredibly satisfied. Sheyna sighed, lazily moistened her lips and opened her eyes to meet his gaze. Her breathing was as quick and winded as his was. He skimmed his hands up her hips, over her waist and then slowly moved them inward to caress her breasts. She drew a shuddering breath.

"I can't get enough of you," he whispered, his pulse hammering in the deep hollow at the base of his throat.

"Me, neither," she replied, wrapping her arms around his neck and moving her hips to hold him close, to keep him within her.

"You want some more?" he asked.

"Yes. I still need you."

"I aim to please," he murmured, smiling as he hardened again. He planted his hands in the bedding on either side of her head and leaned down to kiss her tenderly, thoroughly. She tightened her arms around his neck, and he leaned back and stared down at her. He shifted his position and deepened their union then watched as her eyes widened and her lips parted with a soundless gasp of pleasure.

He moved down, taking a hardened nipple into his mouth, suckling until she moved against him and moaned his name. Releasing her, he gazed up into her amber eyes. "Let's take it slow this time," he murmured.

"I want to ride you," she suggested, her grin lusciously wicked.

With a knowing smile he eased down beside her, rolled her on top of him and took her hips back in his hands. He could get used to this, he realized as she straddled him. The waiting was over. And she was worth all the months it had taken to earn it.

This round was even quicker than the last. She stroked him long and hard and within minutes she shuddered and arched as she contracted around him, pulling him deeper and he came right behind her.

"You're an amazing woman, Sheyna Simmons."

His words made her heart flutter and she raised her head slightly, looked into his eyes then replied, "You're not so bad yourself." There was so much more she wanted to say but she knew revealing her feelings would be a mistake.

Jace smoothed his fingers across her hips and buttocks and dropped a light kiss to her forehead. "I'm looking forward to enjoying the day sightseeing in Las Vegas, but right now I just want to be here in this bed, holding you in my arms just a little bit longer."

That was what she wanted, as well. For this special moment to last as long as humanly possible. At this moment she was the happiest she had been in a long time and she also wanted this time to last. Why did she feel that she belonged in his arms forever? She ran her fingers along his jaw, feeling the bristles and wondering what it would take to change his mind about relationships and finding true love. Didn't he realize that real love could heal past hurts?

If only he loved her as she loved him then everything in her world would be perfect. *Yeah, right.* Jace had made his feelings clear from the beginning when he proposed that she surrender herself to him for one weekend with no strings attached.

She shifted her head on his chest and squeezed her eyelids tightly, trying desperately to shut out reality and the heartache she would be faced with once they returned home. "Thanks for everything, Jace. I will never forget this night."

"Neither will I," Jace murmured as he tilted his head to drop a kiss on her forehead.

Chapter 14

Sheyna eventually drifted off to sleep while Jace continued to run his fingers along her curves.

Jace lay beside her with the strong urge to cruise his lips over every inch of her body, but instead he propped his head up with his elbow and stared down at her. She looked so small lying in the massive king-size bed partially wrapped in a sheet. His eyes perused her curvaceous mahogany body that would serve as an erotic dream for any man. Sheyna was slender but voluptuous, her breasts full and round. The fine sheet rested across her lower body, exposing her small waist and one long shapely leg, which was comfortably draped over his.

Sheyna stirred slightly and released a soft moan,

taunting him further. Desire slammed him and he couldn't deny there was an urge to be inside her body again. Staring down at her, he fought the hard thumping of his heart and the future popped into his mind. Why now? Or better yet, why this woman?

He was still overwhelmed by the last several hours. The time was special and a selfish part of him now felt as if she belonged to him. Jace knew that was ridiculous because commitment was not part of their agreement, but that did nothing to change what he was feeling.

While making love, he had called her "baby" and "love," something he'd never done before. That was how he knew that what had happened between them was special and deep.

Was it love?

Damn. There was that word. A strange sensation twisted through him. He wasn't sure because he'd only loved once, or had thought himself in love once. Only, what he had experienced with Julia wasn't anything like what he was experiencing now with Sheyna. Was he really falling in love this time? And if so, how had Sheyna managed to get past his resistance and touch his heart?

With a frown Jace told himself he was mistaking lust for something deeper, but he wasn't so sure. Love was the last thing he needed to be feeling. Any other time he would have run away kicking and screaming, but with Sheyna he didn't feel quite as resistant.

Jace shifted slightly so that he could take a closer look at her. He loved looking at Sheyna, watching the rise and fall of her breasts as she slept. He couldn't get enough of touching her. He felt himself growing hard again. He hadn't satisfied his hunger and wasn't sure if he ever would.

Bending his head, Jace pressed his lips to the corner of her mouth, pleased that it instantly turned upward. Traveling over to the other side caused her to murmur something incoherent, then she wiggled her hips, rubbing her warm core against his thigh. With an agonized groan Jace drew back, smiled and watched as her eyelids slowly opened. "And that's what a good-morning kiss should be," he said, softly brushing a hand across her smooth cheek.

"Jace," she whispered, her smile curving dreamily.

His loins tightened and in that moment he'd have taken her again if he hadn't heard a knock at the door. Room service.

Reluctantly, he rose, reached for his boxers and moved to the door. A few minutes later he returned to find Sheyna still lying in the exact same spot, only she was wide-awake.

"Breakfast is served."

Sitting up with her back propped against pillows and the headboard, she considered the meal he'd placed in front of her with wide eyes. There was coffee, orange juice, bacon, eggs, English muffins and breakfast potatoes. "Goodness, Jace, how in the world am I going to eat all of this?"

"I'm going to help you," he declared, filling the little china cup with coffee for her. "I figured the two of us worked up quite an appetite last night."

"Oh, really? Are we fishing for compliments this morning?" Sheyna teased as she reached for the grape jelly and spread it over one of the muffins.

"Not at all. You lying in my arms was all the validation I needed."

She giggled then crooked her finger. "Come here, handsome, and I'll show you how much last night meant to me."

He lowered himself onto the bed beside her and she seared him with a hot, lingering kiss. Jace pulled back and winked. "Now, eat. You keep kissing me that way, you might need your energy back a little bit sooner than you intended."

"Yes, sir," she said with a nod, then pulled up the sheet so it covered her bare chest. Even covered he could see her chocolate nipples through the thin white material. He groaned silently and dropped his gaze as he reached for a slice of bacon. He could already see that keeping his hands off her was not going to be easy.

"What do we have planned for today? I hope we can

find some time to do a little shopping," she added, picking up her fork. "I heard you can get some really good deals down here."

"Shopping?" he groaned. "How about we do a little sightseeing?" With a mother and a sister who were both addicted shoppers, the last thing he wanted to do was spend hours in the stores.

She simply shrugged. "I can always go shopping on my own."

There was no way he was letting her out of his sight for several hours. "I think we can compromise." He reached for a muffin then rose from the bed. "Finish eating, I'm going to go and run you a bath." He reached for a copy of *USA Today* the waiter had given him and laid it on the bed beside her.

"Hmm, a hot bath sounds wonderful," she purred, causing his loins to stir again. "Are you planning to join me?"

He glanced over his shoulder and saw the hunger burning in her eyes. If he got in the tub with her there would be no way to restrain himself. "Sure, baby. Anything you want."

In the marble bathroom he turned on the water and added a sprinkling of the bath salts he found on the counter. He then walked to his room and decided to brush his teeth and shave while the water ran and she enjoyed her breakfast.

* * *

Sheyna's eyes followed him out of the room with her heart pounding against her ribs. *God, I love that man.*

Shaking it off, she reached for an English muffin and took a bite. She had to stay focused and she wasn't about to read any more into their relationship than he was offering. It didn't matter because she was no more interested in a committed relationship with him than he was with her.

Liar.

Okay, maybe she was lying to herself. Clearly the smartest thing to do would be to keep her head on straight and then, when the time was right, act as if nothing had happened before someone got hurt.

She heaved a heavy sigh because in her heart she knew it was already too late for that. The physical attraction between her and Jace was stronger than anything she'd ever experienced before. Reaching for her orange juice she tried to wash down the muffin that felt lodged in her throat. It was more than lust and she didn't know how after the night they had shared they were to go back to just being friends. Deep in her heart she knew their relationship would never be the same again.

Jace returned to Sheyna's bathroom and turned the water off. When he walked back into Sheyna's bedroom, she had finished eating and was standing wrapped in the sheet. Her nipples strained against the white fabric, just as Jace strained against his boxers. She dropped the sheet onto the bed and moved toward him with the slow seductive sway of her hips that he loved so much. His gaze moved over every inch of her, from her face to her breasts to her flat stomach to the curve of her hips.

"You'd better go take a bath," Jace muttered, sweat breaking out on his forehead, "before I make love to you again."

She smiled as she moved toward him. "Don't you mean *we'd* better get in the water?"

"What?" he hadn't heard her. He was too busy watching her breasts bounce with each step.

She closed in on him, pressing her breasts to his bare chest. "I said I wanted you to join me."

"I thought you were just joking," he barely managed around a swallow.

"I would never joke about sharing a bath together."

She let her fingers drift downward, down to the waistband of his boxers and started to lower them over his hips. "You're taking a bath with me." She laughed at his raised brow. "And I'm taking your clothes off."

For Sheyna it sure was a treat to strip this man bare. She'd thought about it from the moment he'd stepped out of the bathroom. The shorts landed at his feet. Then she took a tiny step back to admire his powerful shoulders and down his muscular arms to his large erection. With her heart in her throat she ran her hands down his chest. Chocolate, smooth and ripped, with just the perfect amount of hair. She reached for his hand and led him into the adjoining bathroom.

"I take bathing together seriously, you know," she told him as she stepped into the bathtub, the hot water assaulting her skin as she sat down.

Jace followed and sat opposite her. "Sounds good to me. I never use my tub at home. I'd rather shower because it's quicker."

"I love taking baths. It gives me a chance either to catch up on some pleasure reading or simply to relax."

Jace reached for the bar of soap and, without the aid of a washcloth, he lathered his hands. Leaning back in the tub, Sheyna waited, her heart thumping with anticipation. This was such complete madness—where they were, what they were doing, how she felt about him—but she wouldn't have it any other way. She swallowed hard because she wasn't being totally honest with herself. There was one thing she wished that she could change about this entire weekend but she pushed that thought aside because there was no point in dwelling on it and ruining an almost perfect moment.

He started with her toes, massaging them slowly and gently until she released the breath she'd been holding.

He moved up to her ankles and calves. The water was hot and the aromatherapy salts in the bath were making her a little light-headed.

He then moved up to her knees and thighs. He started with her outer thighs, then he shifted and moved to her inner thighs, climbing higher until he was poised at her soft, feminine folds. Sheyna sucked air between her teeth, anticipating his fingers parting her, traveling deeper to find the opening to her body. But instead he climbed higher, obviously intent on teasing her before giving her the pleasure of release.

His strokes were slow and strong. So many times he came close to her. So many times he played in her hair then lowered to the sensitive area below and almost touched her where she needed to feel his hand most, before, to her frustration, he moved away.

Sheyna couldn't stand the teasing a second longer and uttered a faint, "Please, Jace…" and rocked her hips forward, trying to urge his fingers to do more than play.

Jace's hot gaze traveled from her hardened nipples to her face. "Please what, Sheyna?"

"Touch me there, please," she said barely above a whisper.

"All right, baby. Open your legs for me."

Sheyna gasped, her core throbbing as she opened her legs wide.

"You are so beautiful, Sheyna."

Her mouth was dry. Her skin tingled with anticipation. When she was on the verge of screaming, she finally felt his hand slide past the fine curly hair and slide between her folds. She cried out and let her head drop to one side as he entered her. Jace made her feel so damn good. He knew what he was doing. He knew a woman's body and what it took to get her off. With expert precision, he caressed her clit with his thumb while he slid his middle finger deep inside her.

Sheyna opened her legs wider, rocking against his hand until she was whimpering her intense pleasure. "No more," she managed. "Please."

"Please what? Sheyna, baby, tell me what you want."

"No more of this. I want you." She searched the water wildly, grabbed on to his erection and squeezed. "I want this inside me. *Now!*"

"Show me how you want it."

Sheyna rose from the tub, trying her damndest not to slip and fall as she raced into the other room for the box of condoms she had packed in her suitcase. As soon as she tore one off, she hurried back into the bathroom. Climbing into the tub, she pushed him back against the beige porcelain tub and straddled him, then slowly rolled it onto his hard length.

Sheyna positioned herself over his erection and lowered herself onto him slowly. She cried out as his thickness filled her. Jace cursed under his breath then thrust his hips upward. His hands reached down and grabbed her hips and his fingers dug into her flesh while he guided her up and down, himself in and out. The movement was rough, hard and wonderful, and Sheyna could hardly breathe.

Water splashed over the side of the tub, but neither of them noticed. Jace reached for her breasts, and tweaked her nipples as she rode him. She moaned at the intensity. As she rose and lowered against him, his tongue worked her nipples until she was beyond frustration. Pulsing heat grew and grew and she wriggled and smashed her hips onto his lap as she moved back and forth. Then suddenly, whimpering sounds came from her lips just as her body jerked and spasms erupted.

"Jace!" She cried out his name again and again, over and over, and heard Jace curse then growl deep in his throat. He grabbed on to her hips and roughly guided her up and down over his erection, pumping rapidly into her until she had milked him dry.

Finally, she dropped to his chest, her breathing labored. Jace wrapped his arms around her, kissed her neck and whispered loving words in her ear.

Later that morning Sheyna and Jace met with their staff and conducted the two-hour sexual-harassment training session before they left for lunch. Their time together showed no sign of ending when Jace suggested they soak up some sun and take in the sights before dinner. Hand in hand they strolled down the Strip on a perfect autumn afternoon, dipping into the Venetian Hotel to visit Madam Tussaud's Wax Museum. Next they walked through several hotels as they headed to Caesar's Palace to watch the moving statues.

Sheyna was in awe of the award-winning restaurants, out-of-this-world shopping and the eye-popping decor. Jace was patient enough to allow her to dip into one shop after another to look at purses, hats and other accessories. To Sheyna, it felt like more than two friends spending time together while enjoying easy conversation; it felt like they were a couple.

"I can't believe it has taken me this long to come here," Sheyna said as they passed a large chocolate fountain. "This place has everything you could ever need."

Jace smiled down at her. "It's a world-class playground. Why do you think millions of people come to Vegas?"

"To get married," she replied as they strolled through Caesar's Palace past the fourth wedding they'd seen that afternoon. She could see how Las Vegas reigned as the world's wedding capital. Everything you needed was right at your fingertips.

"All these weddings, we'd better get back before the bug rubs off on us," Jace said jestingly.

"Nah, when I get married I plan on doing it at my church with my loved ones around."

Tilting his head, he smiled. "And I'm sure you're gonna have exactly what you want."

She fought against a deep yearning to share that moment with him. "I wouldn't have it any other way," she said softly.

They continued to stroll through the hotel, swinging their arms to the tune of "The Wedding March" while they laughed.

They paused to stare at the moving statutes and waited until the end of the show, then Jace tugged her down the street to New York, New York. "You want to ride the roller coaster?"

Sheyna squinted into the sun as she looked up at the ride on top of the hotel. "You know I do." She raced him inside and within minutes they were in line. While they waited, Jace moved up behind her and wrapped his arms around her midsection. Her lids closed and her lips parted. This was one moment she wanted to hold on to forever. As if he was feeling the same way, he slowly turned her around, lowered his head and pressed his lips to hers.

"I think that should hold me over until later," he replied when he finally came up for air.

After the roller-coaster ride, Jace covered her hand with his and held on to it all the way back to their suite at the hotel.

"We have reservations so you've got one hour to get ready." He dropped a searing kiss to her lips. "Don't keep me waiting."

She smiled, feeling flirtatious. "You can always come in after me."

"I intend to," he replied, and followed her through the bedroom and into the shower.

Why did one man have to look so good? She had looked forward all day to Cirque du Soleil and dinner, but now all she could think about was getting back to their room, lying in Jace's arms and having him inside of her.

"How did you like the show?"

Sheyna looked across the dinner table at him, her eyes wide. She had left the theater in awe. Cirque du Soleil was a modern circus without animals. Live music, colorful costumes. She had been glued to her seat at the amazing performances. The acts included contortionists, jugglers, clowns and trapeze artists. "Wonderful. I've never seen anything like that before."

"Would you like to go out for drinks after dinner?" Jace suggested.

She shook her head.

"What would you like to do?"

"I've got a few ideas," she purred, and gazed across the table from behind lowered eyelids.

"Really?" he asked, lust radiating from the depths of his eyes.

She nodded and Jace signaled the waiter for the check.

Chapter 15

Jace stood on the balcony of his suite and stared at the lights of Las Vegas. He took a swig from the bottle of water he'd grabbed from the minibar and closed his eyes as the cold liquid slid down his throat. It was well past midnight but sleep wasn't coming anytime soon. Making love to Sheyna had touched him in more ways than he'd ever imagined.

Staring at the lights flashing before him, he asked himself for the umpteenth time what it was about that woman that got to him. Sure, she was beautiful and sexy with an in-your-face attitude that he adored, but it was something else. That stubborn pride. Her delicious lips and possibly the way she came apart in his arms.

He blew out a long breath and felt his groin tightening in his boxers. What was it? She was messing with his mind, tearing down the wall, trying to penetrate his heart. This was just supposed to be a weekend fling. But inside he was torn by a different emotion. His heart began to pound wildly making it hard to breathe. A war was going on in his brain that he fought to control. Sheyna penetrated his mind and made him feel things. Maybe the reason he wanted her was that he knew he could never have her. They were too much alike, which made their being together impossible. He wasn't her type and she wasn't his. Or was she?

He squeezed his eyes shut. He didn't want to think about Sheyna or what she was doing to him. He only wanted to enjoy their time together. When they returned to Sheraton Beach, he would face the reality that she was not his woman. They were not a couple, and he had no claims on her. But for now he was going to savor the moment and enjoy having her in his arms.

Tilting his head he finished the bottle then headed toward the room, anxious to make love to Sheyna again.

She walked out of the room and was met by the smell of brewing coffee and the sight of Jace sitting on the couch reading the morning paper. On the table was a tray with an assortment of Danishes and fruit.

Looking down at Jace, she surveyed his legs topped

by a pair of khaki shorts, emphasizing his muscular thighs. Stretching, she released a moan.

Jace lowered the paper at the sound and flashed a warm smile. "Good morning, sleepyhead."

She smiled then moved over to sit on the couch beside him.

"I had them bring up room service."

"So I see." She curled her legs beneath her short night-shirt then kissed him. The scent of soap lingered on his skin, indicating he had just taken a shower. "Mmm." Reaching toward the coffee table, she poured herself a cup of coffee and popped a green grape into her mouth.

He gathered her into his arms, holding her gently and making her his prisoner. "What do you want to do today?"

"I don't know," she began as she leaned back against him. "Maybe shopping?"

He groaned as he released her. "Please, no more shopping."

Laughing she swung around to face him. "Okay, then what do you have in mind?"

"Oh, I can think of a few things," he teased.

"You're just nasty," she murmured, then pressed her lips to his. "I'd better go shower or we'll never get out of here."

Sheyna shared a few more bites of breakfast with him before climbing into the shower where she quickly became aware of all the places her body was sore after their morning lovemaking.

She'd never realized that lovemaking could be so special with someone who cared enough to know how you were feeling, as well. Jace made sure that she was satisfied before he found his own pleasure. He made her feel like the most beautiful woman alive as he delightfully explored every inch of her body.

A sob rose to her throat. She loved him.

Afterward, she pulled out a green sundress she had bought the day before and slipped into it. Standing in front of the mirror, she was amazed and pleased to see that it fitted all of her curves, stopping midthigh.

As she combed through her damp hair, Jace emerged from his room dressed and ready to go and all she could do was stand back and admire him. He was fine as hell and had a body that she could spend the entire afternoon admiring.

"You look fabulous," he said as he moved over and planted a kiss on her lips. "With you showing off those gorgeous legs of yours, I'm going to be fighting all kinds of men off this afternoon."

She giggled. "You're silly."

"Nah, just crazy about you and I have no intentions of sharing you with anyone."

"Why is that?" she dared to ask as she stared up into his eyes.

"Because you belong to me."

At that moment there was an explosion inside her chest.

* * *

Sheyna was still thinking about his confession when they arrived at the buffet in the hotel for lunch. She'd barely heard anything else he said or remembered anything he told her as they took a complete quick tour of the hotel. All she could think about were his words. Did he really mean what he'd said?

She didn't think so, yet for some crazy reason she felt all warm inside at the idea of belonging to him. What she should have done was made it clear that she didn't belong to anyone, instead she had been tongue-tied. This was their last night in Las Vegas and she wanted to make it extra special.

"We're scheduled to meet with five candidates in the morning."

She frowned. "Five! Goodness, you're trying to fry my brains."

"You'll be fine. We'll start at eight o'clock. They'll go through two rounds of interviews, meeting with either you or me first then we'll switch."

She nodded as she chewed a buttery roll. "What time are we leaving tomorrow?"

"Why? Are you in a rush to go home?" he asked between sips of lemonade.

No, because our time together will come to an end. "Just curious if I'll have enough time to rest up before returning to work on Tuesday."

"Why don't you take a few days off? You deserve it," he suggested, then reached for his knife and cut his chicken breast in two.

She'd been dying to paint her spare bedroom. A couple of days off would give her plenty of time. "I think I'll take you up on that offer."

He nodded and appeared pleased by her answer. "Good. We have second-shift training scheduled for this evening, but for now, let's forget about work and concentrate on us."

His words were music to her ears.

Early the next morning, Jace pulled her snugly into his arms and pressed his lips to her forehead. Sheyna rested comfortably in his arms as she felt the heat from his mouth travel down to her chest. She loved this man. She had given him her mind, body and soul and they were his to keep if he wanted.

The shock of how deeply she loved the man holding her in his arms had her clinging tightly to him as her heart pounded heavily against her rib cage. Experience and past relationships had taught her just how unwise it was to give her heart to a man, but ever since Jace had decided to pursue what was happening between them, caution had flown out the window with a part of her brain. She couldn't think straight, and the fact that she had not only given her heart but her body to a man who would never love her back scared her to death.

Shifting on the bed, she pressed her lips to his, desperately needing what they were experiencing to last as long as possible. As he deepened the kiss, her lips trembled, then parted, inviting him to explore deeper. When the kiss finally ended, she rested her head on his chest again and allowed the tears to flow freely. In a couple of hours they would be heading back to Sheraton Beach and their weekend in Las Vegas would be nothing more than a memory.

Chapter 16

Sheyna moved to a booth at the back of the deli where Brenna was waving her hand in the air, trying to get her attention.

"Hey, you," Sheyna said as she slid onto the bench across from her friend.

"Hey, yourself. How was your trip?"

It took everything she had not to reveal her innermost feelings. "Great," she replied, then quickly changed the subject. "I know you didn't ask me to meet you for lunch just so you could drill me about my weekend in Las Vegas. So what's going on?" she asked inquisitively.

"We're pregnant."

"Ooh! Congratulations," Sheyna squealed, then sprang

from her seat and moved around to hug her best friend. "I'm so happy for you. Have you told Jabarie yet?" she asked when she returned to the other side of the table.

As she leaned back, Brenna's eyes danced with excitement. "Actually he's the one who told me. That man knows my cycle better than I do."

"I am so happy for you. Jabarie's parents are going to be so excited."

Brenna nodded in agreement. "We're going to tell them this weekend. Speaking of my mother-in-law… she asked me to invite you to dinner this Thursday."

Sheyna's jaw dropped. "You're kidding!"

"Nope, I think she really likes you."

Sheyna snorted, finding that hard to believe. "I'll have to think about that," she mumbled, then glanced down at the table.

"Now I'm dying to hear what happened in Las Vegas."

Sheyna sighed. She had been avoiding Brenna's calls since she and Jace had returned because she didn't want to have to talk about her feelings. She took a deep breath. Just as she had expected, things were back to normal. She hadn't heard from Jace since he had dropped her off at her house. She missed him like crazy but refused to pick up the phone. "We had a wonderful time doing touristy things."

Brenna stared at her impatiently as if wondering if she was going to tell her any more than that. When moments passed and Sheyna didn't say anything else, Brenna asked bluntly, "Did you sleep with him?"

Sheyna let her jaw drop. "Excuse me…"

Brenna tapped one manicured fingernail on the table. "Well…did you?"

Heat coursed through her at the memories. She picked up the menu and pretended to study it. "You're being nosy."

"And you're avoiding the question," Brenna spat as she snatched the menu away. There was no tease in her voice.

"Okay, yes, I slept with him. So what?"

Brenna lifted her gaze to match Sheyna's, arching an eyebrow. "Are the two of you a couple now?"

Oh, how I wish that were true. Sheyna leaned back in her chair and sighed. She was done surrendering. She had agreed to a weekend fling and in exchange she'd got a weekend she'd never forget. However, along with it came heartache. At this point, any hopes for a future with him were over. Nevertheless, she wouldn't be forgetting the time they had shared anytime soon.

She took a sip of her water before speaking. "No, we had an understanding and went into the weekend without expecting anything from each other, and I wouldn't have had it any other way."

The waitress arrived and Sheyna was grateful for the interruption. She ordered tuna on whole wheat while Brenna ordered a salad. The waitress had barely moved to the next table when Brenna barked, "You mean to tell me you're both going to act like nothing happened?"

"Basically." She nodded, moving her gaze to the window and making a point of studying the traffic outside.

"Tell me why." She could feel Brenna's eyes on her. "Especially since I know that isn't what you want."

Sheyna frowned. "Why would you say that?" Their gazes finally met as she waited for her best friend to explain.

"Because you're in love with him."

Sheyna said nothing, instead avoided her friend's probing eyes. Sheyna knew she loved Jace. Brenna knew she loved him. So why couldn't he love her back? She'd rather leave it alone instead of dredging up the past weekend and making it harder to function, but she needed someone to talk to about it. "I still haven't told him how I feel."

"Why not? Maybe that's all it will take for the two of you to finally come to terms with what you're both feeling." She reached for her water glass and said as an afterthought, "He was over last night. I was coming into the kitchen and I heard him mention your name to Jabarie."

"Really, what did he say?"

"They stopped talking when they heard me coming but Jabarie told me last night that Jace has really been acting strangely lately, and he knows it has a lot to do with you."

Her heart soared. How wonderful it would be to

know that he felt the same way about her, but she had sense enough not to get her hopes up.

"I thought you didn't want me getting involved with Jace? He's a heartbreaker, remember?"

"Well, it's a little late for that now." Brenna searched her face. "I just don't want to see you get hurt."

It was definitely too late for *that*. Her heart was already deeply involved.

Reaching across the table, Brenna took Sheyna's hand and stared over at her. "If you want that man, then go get him."

Instantly, Sheyna shook her head. "No way. I'm not running after him."

"You don't have to, girl. Show him how we women do." She wagged her eyebrows suggestively. "Show that man what you're working with." She leaned back on the bench and folded her arms across her chest. "Jace is used to women who let him run and dictate the relationship. It's time for someone to turn the tables on him. Show him that he can't always have things his way. That you have the power to control the relationship, as well."

Sheyna took a moment to think about what Brenna said, and finally her lips curled downward stubbornly.

The weekend had been a total surrender. Jace had made love to her in every room of the suite. He had proven that passion ran deep between them. Their weekend in Las Vegas had been beautiful. It didn't take long for her to realize her life would never be the same.

As much as she wanted Jace in her life permanently, there was no way she was running after him. He would have to make the first move. "Not this time. If Jace wants me, then he's going to have to show me. I'm not the one running from love. He is."

Brenna blew out a frustrated breath. "The two of you are just too stubborn. Why play games when you don't have to?"

"Who's playing games? I made it perfectly clear to Jace what I was looking for."

"I hope you're right because we're running out of time."

Her brow drew together. "Out of time for what?"

Brenna gave her a hard look as though Sheyna should have known what she was talking about. "Our children are supposed to be growing up together, which means you are a couple of months behind. It's time to catch up."

She laughed. Leave it to Brenna to find a way to put a smile on her face. Marrying Jace and having his children was exactly what she wanted to do, but the ball was now in his court.

Jace watched through the glass wall as Sheyna conducted an interview. It was amazing to watch her in action. He smiled. She was good at what she did. His chest tightened with…something.

She had been off the last few days and not seeing her had started to drive him crazy. He'd wanted so badly to call her, but thought it best to try and put some distance between them. But he could no longer stay away. A shudder passed through his chest as he realized how much he'd missed her and how she had constantly been in his thoughts since their return. He wanted not only to hold her, he couldn't wait to make love to her again.

He brushed a hand down his face. For the last few days, his mind had been in turmoil. It was so unlike him to be caught up over a woman. Why was she so hard to let go of? What made her so different from all the rest?

Staring through the glass, he studied her. She was indeed beautiful. Her hair was combed back away from her smooth mahogany face, displaying prominent features that took his breath. Her long neck made him want to kiss her there. He licked his lips then let out a long breath to slow his desire. The way her blouse clung to her breasts did strange things to him.

Did he want her to be his?

That question shook him hard. Their time together in Las Vegas had brought his feelings to the forefront. Now they were back and everything was supposed to have returned to normal. Two friends, working together.

He dragged a frustrated hand through his hair. He didn't need this type of frustration. Their eyes met and his heart leaped. Quickly, he shifted his attention and strode down the hall to his office.

"How was your interview?"

Sheyna looked up from the report on her desk to find Jace standing in her doorway, hands buried deep in his pockets. Her heart pounded. Her body yearned for his touch. She scrunched up her nose. "He was a candidate who needed to reschedule. Fresh out of school. Very little experience. If he's really serious about working here I think an entry-level position would be ideal for him. In the meantime, I think Harlan and I have agreed to offer Jonathan the chef position."

"Fabulous."

She nodded, pleased with the outcome. "He's coming in on Friday to prepare a meal for the restaurant and if all of his references check out I think we'll have a winner."

Nodding, Jace stepped into the room and shut the door behind him, and then slowly moved over to where she was sitting. Her heart pounded and she found herself rising from her seat and rounding her desk to meet him. As soon as she did, he wrapped an arm around her waist and pulled her against him.

"I've missed you so much," he murmured.

"Yeah? Then show me."

Sheyna knew she wasn't thinking or using her common sense. She knew that being in her office alone with

Jace was a mistake. But she couldn't think straight around him and right now she didn't care about anything other than feeling Jace's mouth against hers.

He cupped the back of her head and she was totally under his spell and more than willing to cooperate. His tongue brushed hers, causing a moan to escape her lips. She had missed this, she had missed *him* so much that tears burned the back of her eyes.

Jace deepened the kiss and she held on, pressing her body firmly against his. She slid her hands over his shoulders and down his back. He was so strong on the outside yet gentle and caring on the inside. *If only he'd let me love him.*

The last two days alone played in her mind, and she held on to him, unsure if this moment would ever happen again, and wanting to take all she could, Sheyna held on, clung to the man she loved—Jace Beaumont.

Jace lifted her onto her desk then shifted so he was standing between her legs. Immediately, she felt his erection. Damn, she wanted him buried inside her. As they prolonged the kiss, her control slipped away from her. Afraid of what was happening between them she pulled back, breaking the contact.

Still standing between her thighs, he was staring down at her. Eyes burning with desire, he caused her to shudder.

"What was that for?" she asked around a shaky breath.

"What do you think?"

She stared at him until the meaning was clear. A warm feeling rushed through her veins. She closed her eyes and inhaled the scent of his cologne. Before she could find the words to respond, he took her hand and led her out the office.

"Sheyna, your three o'clock appointment is running late."

"Cancel her appointments. Ms. Simmons will be out for the rest of the afternoon." Before she could protest, Jace lured her down the hall past the staffs' prying eyes and up the elevator to the executive suite on the eleventh floor. She was so stunned she couldn't find her voice to speak.

At the end of the hall, Jace punched in the security code, then swung her into his arms then kicked the door open. Sheyna was laughing so hard she was in tears. He carried her over to the bed and dropped her down onto the plush comforter then he reached for his belt buckle.

"I guess you plan to take advantage of me this afternoon."

He tossed off his suit jacket and joined her on the bed. "Something like that."

Her tongue went deep, stroking his as he kissed her passionately, and she slid her hands over him, feeling his body, all hard, lean planes and corded muscles. Excitement exploded in every nerve of her body. As he trailed kisses along her throat, his hands peeled away her blouse. Her bra went with it. While she unfastened his slacks, he cupped her breasts, looking down at her. His fingers were warm, setting her aflame.

He quickly finished peeling off his clothes and then hers.

Jace held her in his arms and joy raced through her blood as she felt the heat of his skin against hers. His chest hairs tickled her back, his erection, hard and ready against her buttocks. He ran wet kisses along the side of her neck and ears and she moaned, then hungrily wriggled against him, hoping to feel him inside her body where he belonged.

"Sheyna, tell me what you want," he uttered, his voice tight with restraint.

"You. Just you."

He groaned. "You'll always have me." His magic words were as passionate as his caresses. He reached to his pants for a condom and rolled it on, then he stroked his hand between her thighs. She moaned his name, dying to feel him inside her. He nudged her legs apart and eased his erection into her just an inch, then gripped her shoulders and sank deep inside her body.

Sheyna could barely catch her breath, she could hardly think. But instinct had her moving, had her following Jace as he stroked. His hands left her shoulders and slipped around, grazing her breasts, then through her curls to the aching center of her. Sheyna sucked air through her teeth in response. Slowly and readily, he worked her, his thrusts making her wet, his caresses making her moan.

It didn't take long before Sheyna's legs began to tremble, and with one flick of his thumb across her clit, she cried out, then came apart against his hand.

As she was met by one orgasm and then another, she continued to pump her hips back and soon it was Jace whose breathing changed.

"I can't get enough!" he moaned.

"Of what?" she moaned against the pillow.

"This. Us," he cried, and he pumped harder and faster, slamming against her buttocks.

"Jace…"

But Jace was in ecstasy. He called out her name repeatedly and he slammed against her almost violently while his hands held on steadily to her hips. Finally, he collapsed onto the bed and rolled her over against him. Holding her tightly in his arms, he rained kisses along her back and arm.

"You are something else, Sheyna Simmons," he whispered.

She hugged his arms, loved the weight of his body beside her. "I'm sure you say that to all your women."

"No, only to you. You make me feel things I've never felt before, Sheyna. Weak, vulnerable, and after not seeing you for the last few days, crazy." He buried his face in her hair. "Do you know what I'm saying?"

"Yes, I do." Weak and vulnerable were two emotions she also felt, only she wasn't trying to fight them.

"What are we going to do?" he whispered against her hair.

"Not we, Jace," she said gently. "You. I've been honest from the beginning about what I wanted in a relationship, and after our weekend together it should be more than obvious what I want. I'm not afraid to admit my feelings for you or where I would like this relationship to go."

Jace said nothing. Instead, he pulled her snugly into his arms and rested his head comfortably on the pillow beside her. For a moment, she thought to say something else but then thought it best to leave things alone. It was up to Jace to decide where their relationship went from here.

Chapter 17

The following afternoon Sheyna was still as confused as ever. The mixed signals were starting to drive her crazy. Yesterday, after their spontaneous union in the suite, she had gone home alone and spent most of the evening waiting by the phone for Jace to call. That morning, he had finally called when she had barely rolled out of bed to invite her to his house that night for dinner. The thought still had her stomach churning with excitement.

After lunch, Sheyna arrived back at her desk to a stack of applications that her secretary had left. *A manager's job is never done,* she thought, followed by a sigh as she lowered herself onto her seat. She stuck her purse in her bottom drawer then slipped her pumps off her feet. She had spent her lunch hour shopping. She gave a wicked smile as she thought about how she had spent the entire hour at a lingerie boutique downtown, shopping for something sexy. Tonight when she arrived at Jace's house, she wanted to be daring and sexy, and the little black number she planned to wear beneath her trench coat was just that.

Her body still hummed from Jace's lovemaking the afternoon before and her stomach quivered as she thought about him scooping her into his arms and carrying her off to bed. She couldn't wait to feel his lips on her, or better yet, feel him making love to her once again.

Reaching into a plastic bag, she removed the catfish platter she had picked up at Clarence's Chicken and Fish House on Main Street on her way in. As she opened the container, the smell of hot sauce and grease tickled her nose. She brought a nugget to her lips and took a bite.

"Ooh!" she groaned. Nobody made fish like old man Clarence. He'd been a fixture in their small town for longer that she'd been living.

Noticing the morning's newspaper on the end of her desk she reached for it and flipped through the pages while she ate. Halfway through she stopped and grabbed a diet soda out of her small refrigerator before returning to her seat. As she reached the entertainment section her eyes caught Carren's picture next to her weekly article. The caption read, Beware of Playboys. Sheyna had never been a big fan of Carren's articles, which to her read like a weekly blog, but there was no way she could ignore what Carren had written.

Her hand stalled, holding a piece of fish as she read. The article sounded like a woman scorned. Weekend seduction. No strings attached and the three-week rule. Was she talking about Jace? Her stomach tightened. How long had it been since the two of them started their fling? It would be two weeks on Saturday. Would their relationship end, as well? She slumped back on the chair. *Of course it will.* What in the world made her think she was any different from Carren, Penelope, Tiffany and all the others?

Sheyna suddenly lost her appetite and dropped the fish back into the container and pushed it away. What a fool she had been to think that things between them would be any different.

Leaning back in her chair, she took a ragged breath. Who was she fooling? Jace had made it clear from the jump that he wasn't looking for a commitment. *So why do I feel like crying?*

Because she loved him and somehow she had decided to settle for whatever he was willing to give her instead of what she really wanted. Jace's love and commitment. His last name. His babies.

She folded her hands in her lap and thought some more about yesterday. Although they had made love, in reality nothing between them had changed. They were still doing things Jace's way—a fling with no strings. As far as he was concerned, he wanted to have his cake and eat it, too. Although they had made love again and he had invited her to his house for dinner tonight, he hadn't given her any indication that anything between them had changed, and that bothered her more than Carren's article.

A sob caught in her throat. How could she have done this to herself? She loved him but he didn't love her and nothing was ever going to change unless she did something about it.

Her office phone rang and she straightened in her seat and reached for it.

"Sheyna?"

"Daddy?"

"Hey, precious. I just wanted you to be the first person to know, I asked Jennifer to marry me."

She bit back a sob. "Oh, Daddy, that's wonderful."

"Thank you, baby. That means a lot coming from you."

"When are the two of you planning to tie the knot?" Her voice was shakier than she would have liked.

"We're thinking about a quiet ceremony this spring with just our close friends and family around."

"That sounds wonderful."

They chatted a little longer then she ended the call and the tears began to fall heavily.

She wanted exactly what her father had found with Jennifer and she refused to settle for anything less.

Something wasn't right.

Jace stared into what was left of the log he had placed in the fireplace over two hours ago as he tried to figure out why Sheyna still hadn't arrived.

He glanced down at his cell phone on his hip and noted there were no missed calls. He even checked to make sure his ringer was on. The house phone had rung all evening—one person after another who had read Carren's column, but not one call had been from the person he hoped to hear from most, Sheyna Simmons.

He fought the urge to call her again, since it had barely been thirty minutes since his last call to her house and her cell phone. Hell, he'd even called the office just in case she happened to still be there. All three attempts had gone unanswered.

Moving over to the small bar in the corner of what should have been his formal dining room, Jace reached for the bottle of champagne that had been chilling for the last several hours. The ice had long since started to melt. He removed the bottle and poured himself two fingers full of the bubbling liquid.

She isn't coming.

His chest tightened. He had gone all out. Lobster, candlelight, soft music. Speaking of music—with heavy determined steps, he moved over to the stereo and turned the music off. The soft melody was only making him feel worse.

Jace began pacing and muttering to himself. Why hadn't she come? As he sipped the bubbly liquid an obvious thought came to mind. She had read the stupid article.

Bianca had wasted no time carrying the article to his office to read, then she'd told him how disappointed she was before she stalked out of his office. Was he as bad as Carren had painted him to be? Nah, he didn't think so. He'd never promised any of those women anything other than a good time, and when the fun was over it signaled that it was time for him to move on. Now, however, as he thought about it, it made him feel worse than he'd felt when he'd first read the article. Not so much what Carren had said, but that it was so untrue when it came to his relationship with Sheyna. With her there was no three-week rule. He wanted their relationship to last as long as they both enjoyed each other's company. Wasn't that what she wanted, as well?

Glancing down at his watch again he started pacing around the living room, ready to pull his hair out. What in the world was wrong with him? Since when did he lose his mind over a female? He never sat around waiting for the phone to ring. Yet, he was dying to hear her car pull into his driveway. He was anxious to hold her in his arms and assure her that their relationship was going to be different.

He combed his fingers through his hair. Damn. He couldn't take it any longer. He finished his drink with one swallow, then lowered the flute onto the counter. He hit Redial and called her home and when he got the recording, he tried her cell phone. But instead of calling her office, Jace called her best friend, Brenna. If anyone knew where Sheyna was, she would. He scowled when his brother answered.

"How's it going?" he felt compelled to ask.

"Fine, and you?"

"Not too well. I'm looking for Sheyna. We had a date that she hasn't shown up for."

Jabarie gave a hard laugh. "Can you blame her after that article?"

Jace rubbed a frustrated hand across his head again. "My relationship with Sheyna is nothing like that."

"Does she know that?"

He swore through the receiver. *No, I guess she wouldn't know.*

"If she's not there then I guess she followed your three-week rule and decided to dump you instead," he added with a chuckle. "Sorry, Jace, but you know what they say about what goes around…"

"Yeah, yeah," he retorted. "Have you or Brenna seen her?" he asked, sounding almost desperate.

"She was here earlier, and I overhead her say something to Brenna about going to Wilmington for dinner tonight…with some guy."

He was so angry, he couldn't speak.

"You can't always have things your way," Jabarie said by way of softening the blow.

"I'm crazy about Sheyna."

"Then I guess it's time you proved it to her."

That was exactly what he planned to do.

Chapter 18

Sheyna looked across the table at Jace, who was going over the last of the performance appraisals for the housekeeping department. Her stomach was in knots about the night before.

They'd been sitting here for the last several hours and Jace still hadn't asked where she had been, which only affirmed her decision to end their fling. Although it didn't make her feel any better. Her heart hurt and she had the strong urge to cry, but she refused. Instead they spent the entire afternoon together, business as usual and being too damn professional.

"These look really good," he commented. "Only I would extend Shirley's probationary period ninety more days. Her attendance has improved but she's still been coming in late more often than I would like."

She frowned. "She's been dealing with a sick mother."

"Then you need to enroll her in the Family Medical Leave Act for some time off."

"Fine." She wasn't in the mood to argue. She was too sad to care. Although, he was probably right.

He handed her the file and while she made notes on the outside, he reached for the next on the pile.

While waiting she gnawed on her lips and gazed at the wide shoulders she had rested her head on while she'd dozed off in his arms. Would she ever feel his arms around her again? Maybe not. He didn't seem too upset about last night. It didn't appear to have bothered him at all and that caused her stomach to quiver. Had she given him the out that he needed?

She pushed her pain aside long enough for them to finish the last of the files. Jace commended her on many reviews and gave her constructive criticism and suggestions on others. Jace was kind and professional, he even laughed when the moment permitted, but he made no mention of their relationship or last night. Her heart sank. It was officially over.

He glanced down at his watch. "Well, it's after five. Why don't we call it a night?"

Nodding, she didn't bother to look over at him as she rose from the chair.

"How about we go and grab some dinner?"

Gathering up all her strength, she replied, "I don't think so."

He gave her a surprised look. "Why not?"

Sheyna dropped a frustrated fist to her waist. "Because I don't want to spend the evening with you. It's over between us and we need to keep things strictly professional from here on out."

There was a long pause. "What happened to us at least being friends?"

Her voice cracked at his immediate acceptance that their relationship was over. *Because I'm hopelessly in love with you, you idiot!* "Things can never be the way they once were." She scooped up the folders and looked up at him. For the longest time he just stared at her, and she looked back. Staring into those beautiful eyes, she wanted so badly to drop the files and run into his arms and make him promise never to let her go again. But what they'd had was over, and the sooner she accepted that the better off they would both be.

"Have a good evening." She could feel his eyes on her as she headed toward the door.

"Sheyna!" Jace called after her.

"Yes?" she said as she slowly turned around.

"You want a commitment, right?"

She tilted her brow. "What are you talking about?"

"You want me to tell you I love you and give you a

relationship—a committed relationship," he stated with a slightly bitter edge. He was mad at her for not coming to him last night, and frustrated because he cared so much. He didn't mean to sound so bitter, so resentful. He didn't mean to aim his anger at her. But she was here, and he didn't know what else to do to keep her from walking out on him.

Sheyna obviously wasn't having it. With quick steps she moved back in his direction with her hand to her hip. "Excuse me? But who told you to put words in my mouth?" she snapped.

"Come off it, Sheyna. The reason why you didn't come and see me last night was because you want something that I'm not willing to give you. It's not enough that I can't eat or sleep because I can't stop thinking about you, but you won't be happy until you have my heart, as well."

"I'm not going to bother responding because it's obvious you think you know me better than I know myself. Let me tell you something, Jace, you ain't all that." She swung around, but before she could make it to the door, Jace jumped in front of her.

"Admit it, Sheyna. You want a future with me."

"Okay, so what if I do?" she answered defensively. "Is that so wrong? I love you, Jace Beaumont, but you're too stupid to appreciate that."

His heart pounded. She loved him. Damn! What the

hell was he doing picking a fight with her? He knew what he was doing. It was his way of trying to sabotage what they had. He raked a frustrating hand across his chin and gazed down at her beautiful amber eyes that were now blazing with anger.

"I can't," was all he could manage.

"Fine," she said, and sighed. Obviously, she realized that she was fighting a losing battle because her shoulders sagged with defeat.

"Is that all you have to say?" he asked, flabbergasted.

"What do you want me to do, jump up and down and start crying? Well, I'm not! If you're not interested in having a future with me, then I'll find someone who is."

He stared at her, his heart pounding against his rib cage.

Impatiently, she finally pushed him out of her way and headed to the door. "I feel sorry for you, Jace," she called over her shoulder. "Don't expect me to sit around and wait for you to decide what you want because I won't! I want a husband and babies and that white picket fence, and if you aren't willing to offer me those things, I need to find a man who is." She didn't wait for a response as she exited the room.

Standing at the center of the room, Jace watched the sway of her hips as she moved down the hall, each step taking her farther away from him and his life.

He needed to channel his anger elsewhere because it wasn't her fault he had run her away, looking for the easy way out of their relationship, the same way he had done with all the others. He had sabotaged his own relationship.

He strode to his office, closed the door and lowered himself into his seat. Jace shook his head, suddenly feeling totally disgusted with himself for his behavior. What in the world was he thinking, taking his frustrations out on Sheyna? His mood darkened at the thought. And then he realized he'd never felt so alone in his life.

Sheyna made it home shortly after six, and for once she put her car in the garage because she didn't want anyone—Jace—to know she was home.

In her room, she removed her shoes and carried them over to her walk-in closet, then began changing out of her work clothes. As she unzipped her skirt, images of Jace's face as she remembered it in the conference room flashed in her mind. She saw a stubborn determination to control his own feelings. He couldn't have been any clearer if he'd written it all out. Even though she knew deep down that he cared about her, his rejection still hurt. Obviously he didn't love her, and, as hard as it was to stomach, she had to find a way to accept that because, in all honesty, he hadn't promised her anything other than a weekend she would never forget.

And that's the truth.

He'd made it clear in so many words that he resented

his feelings for her and refused to acknowledge them as a couple, or her love.

Outside her window the trees stirred gently in the breeze as rain blanketed the town. Sheyna lay back on the bed and watched her curtains blowing with the wind. She had to walk away from him when she did because there was no way she was going to stand there, begging and pleading for him to accept what was happening between them. If Jace chose to ignore his feelings, then it was his loss, not hers.

But that didn't stop her from closing her eyes against the tears that threatened to fall as she spent the next hour wondering how she was going to pick up the pieces of her broken heart and get on with her life.

Jace decided to stop by the bar on his way home. He was so upset he didn't know what to do. He was sitting at a table in the corner watching a couple at the next table. It was obvious the two of them were in love. The touching. The looks. Loneliness assailed him and suddenly he was torpedoed with the strong desire to have the same thing. He sat there for the longest time thinking about the last several years of his life, and he had just ordered his second beer when he glanced up to find two big men towering over him. Darnell and Scott. Sheyna's brothers.

"You don't mind if we join you, do you?" Darnell queried, and took a seat before Jace could answer.

"What's going on with you and my sister?" Scott asked as if he were disscussing something as simple as the weather forecast.

Darnell gave Jace a stern look. "I just came from her house and she looked miserable. You wouldn't know anything about that, would you?"

Jace's eyes traveled from one to the other. If they had arrived an hour ago, he might have provided them with a flippant response, but now that he'd had a chance to think and get his head on straight, he realized the only fool at the table was him.

He wanted what his brother, Jabarie, had—someone at home waiting for him when he got there. He had never wanted things like that before. He had prided himself on his willpower to resist loneliness and all those other needy things that made a man finally succumb to marriage. But now that Sheyna was in his life, now that he realized he loved her, those reasons seemed foolish and stupid. He could see why he had fallen in love with Sheyna. He could see why he wanted to spend the rest of his life with her. Who would want to spend their life alone when they could have someone like her in their life? Before her he hadn't given falling in love again any real consideration.

Now he understood why he missed her so much when they were apart and why she filled his thoughts and his heart. He had been in love with her all along, only he was too stubborn to admit it. The realization had his head spinning, and if he'd had more to drink than two beers, he would have sworn he was drunk.

He tried to think of life without her and couldn't. All he could think about was the time they'd spent in Las Vegas. During those days something had happened to him. She'd torn down his resolve and penetrated his heart. She'd made him realize how lonely his life was. Sheyna had filled a void in his life that he'd had no idea existed. And to think he thought he had been in love with Julia! What he'd felt then in no shape or form compared to what he felt now for Sheyna. He'd had no idea he could feel this deeply about a woman. He took a deep, shaky breath. He knew then, without a shadow of a doubt, that he wanted to spend the rest of his life with Sheyna.

"Before you both get bent out of shape, I want you to know that I love your sister and plan to marry her. If she'll have me."

Scott and Darnell exchanged looks before they chuckled.

"Welcome to the family." Darnell gave him a firm handshake while Scott slapped him heartily on the back.

"How about I buy another round?" Jace offered.

Darnell nodded his head. "I can see we're going to get along perfectly."

Chapter 19

Three days later, Sheyna was still sleeping when she heard a heavy banging at her door. Disoriented, she hurried down the hall and swung the door open to find Jace standing on the other side.

"What are you doing here?" she snapped, angry that he'd caught her looking her worst.

"I want to show you something. Get dressed." He held up a bag. "I brought breakfast."

"Maybe I want to spend the morning sleeping late," she replied stubbornly.

He moved over and planted a kiss on her forehead. "You'll have plenty of time to sleep later. Preferably in my arms, but right now I want to show you something."

He handed her a cup of coffee and pointed her in the direction of her room. "You've got fifteen minutes, after that I'm coming in to get you."

Obediently, she moved back down the hall to her bedroom. As she dressed, her heart raced with excitement at what his reasons could be for showing up at her house. Glancing at the clock she saw that it was barely eight. She had no idea where he was taking her, but she was anxious to find out.

"This is where you're taking me?" she asked when they'd arrived at their destination. She couldn't hide her disappointment.

"Yep," Jace replied as he climbed out of the car.

The family-owned farm spread over several acres, with fresh-grown vegetables available in early summer, apple trees and pumpkin patches for little trick-or-treaters. Jace had to admit that apple picking wasn't an ordinary choice for a romantic date, but Sheyna wasn't an ordinary woman and neither was their situation.

After realizing how much he loved Sheyna, he'd spent the last couple of days planning something special. He could have taken her out to dinner or to a movie or a long walk on the beach. Hell, he could have taken her up in a hot-air balloon, but he wanted to do something that would mean a lot to her. Jace hoped this place would be the perfect setting to delve into whatever was happening between them.

"I thought you might like it," he said as he came around the SUV beside her, "but if you don't, we can go someplace else."

"It's fine," she began with a curious look. "I'm interested in seeing where this goes."

He simply shrugged. "I thought maybe the idea would appeal to you."

She narrowed her eyes at him. "What idea?"

"Apple picking."

Her eyes widened. "Apple picking? You?" She started laughing.

"What's so funny?"

Sheyna leaned back on the SUV, sizing him up. "You, picking apples. This I've got to see." She leaned her head back and let out a loud peal of laughter. He sighed with relief, happy to see that at least she wasn't as angry with him as he had originally thought. That was definitely a good sign.

"I wanted to do something that *you* like, for a change. And I remembered you mentioned that you like coming here in the fall and picking apples."

She nodded. "You're so right."

"Besides, maybe you'll make me one of those fabulous apple pies."

She grinned. "I think I can manage that."

"Good." Jace went into the back of his SUV and took out two old wooden buckets he'd picked up the day before. After placing them on the ground, he removed a backpack and tugged it over his shoulders. "Grab a bucket."

She reached for a scarred wooden bucket.

Taking her free hand, he led the way to the neat rows of trees. Knowing the first rows would already be picked over, they traveled deeper until they were all but obscured by the thick, fragrant branches.

Jace and Sheyna walked in silence, allowing the sun and the sweet-smelling breeze to lull them into a comfortable truce.

Sheyna raised her head and took a deep breath, inhaling the scents around her with a sensuous enthusiasm. Watching the unconscious display, he wondered why it had taken him so long to realize how beautiful she was. The way she had his heart thumping against his chest was a clear indication how much he needed this woman in his life. If she'd still have him.

She opened her eyes and caught him staring at her, the desire apparent in his eyes. She didn't turn away, however, but held his gaze, then turned and continued down the secluded path.

He trailed after her, keeping far enough away so that he wasn't tempted to touch her. They reached a couple of trees and there was a ladder leaning against the tallest one. She swung around. "You planned this, right?"

He nodded.

Satisfied by his answer, she lowered her bucket at the bottom of the tree. And started up the ladder. He moved beside her to steady it.

They worked in silence. She used her shirt to hold the apples and when she couldn't handle any more, she slowly came down the ladder, filled the bucket then went up again.

"Would you like me to hold the ladder while you pick some?" she asked.

"No, I'm enjoying watching you."

Nodding, she started picking again while humming a tune he wasn't familiar with.

"The first time I went apple picking, my mother took me. I think I was eight."

He listened as she told him about the mother–daughter time they used to spend together. He had never gotten the chance to meet her mother, but from everything he had heard over the years, he could tell she was an extraordinary woman just like her daughter.

As Sheyna continued to talk about her apple-picking days and the first time she bit into an apple to discover a worm, Jace smiled, pleased to find that it was still easy for them to talk to each other. Whatever else had changed between them, they still had that.

But he wanted more.

When both buckets were filled, he carried them along the path until they got too heavy.

"Let's make a pit stop, down by the lake," Jace suggested.

Though she wasn't sure what exactly he was up to, Sheyna followed him toward the gently lapping water. They were at a crossroads in their relationship and she was interested in seeing where things went from here. So far, it appeared that Jace was willing to do whatever he had to do to salvage their friendship and she was grateful for that, even though deep in her heart she wanted so much more.

Near the lake, he took a blanket from his backpack. After spreading it on the grass, he pulled out a bottle of orange juice, blueberry muffins, bacon and fresh fruit. He lowered himself and poured her a glass of juice.

She sat on the blanket beside him and took the drink he offered. "You're something else."

"I'll take that as a compliment."

"I'm not sure I meant it as one."

He smiled, not insulted, and crossed his legs. "Care to explain?"

"Not really. It's just a way to remind myself that I need to keep my guard up around you."

There was a noticeable pause before Jace replied, "You know I would never hurt you."

But you already have. Couldn't he see her heart was broken? "Not intentionally," she managed to say.

He lifted his glass in a toast. "To good times."

"To good times," she agreed, tapping her glass against his. She wondered how many more she would get to share with him before he tired of her, too. Gosh, she was such a fool. She had made a vow to stay away from Jace, and here she was acting like a lovesick puppy out picking apples with him as if nothing had happened between them.

She sipped her juice to keep from crying. She had to admit, for romance, the setting was perfect. But she wasn't about to fall for the ambiance. She was well beyond that. She loved him and always would, no matter what else happened between them, but she was not going to let him play with her emotions any further.

Sheyna looked up in time to catch him staring at her, and before she could respond, Jace leaned over, then paused, giving her plenty of time to retreat, but she couldn't, not when she loved him as much as she did. Instead she closed her eyes and leaned into his kiss. Once again sparks flew and she gave freely to the passion of his kiss. His mouth covered hers hungrily, and when he leaned her back against the blanket, she willingly obeyed. Jace could have made love to her right out in the countryside, beneath the clouds, and she would have allowed him. A sob caught in her throat. *What a fool you are.*

Quickly, before she did further damage, she broke off the kiss and pushed hard against his chest. "Listen, Jace, that part of our relationship is over."

Reaching out, he caressed her face. "I can't accept that."

His comment angered her. "This isn't a game!" she barked. "This is my heart you're playing with."

He rose then reached for her hand. "I'm not playing a game. Come on. I want to show you something."

She was ready to be alone. "Can we just go back to your Tahoe?"

"In a minute. I need to show you something first. Please." There was no way she could say no to the pleading look in his eyes.

She swallowed hard and squared her shoulders. "Fine, but no more kisses."

His smile returned. "I promise I won't touch you unless you ask me to."

Leaving behind their picnic, Jace took her hand and led her farther down the path through the small woods. The trees were a mix of red dogwoods and oak trees that covered the vast area. Her heart pounded with a combination of yearning and anger. Her whole being seemed to fill with waiting. She had no idea what he was up to, but one thing she knew, her heart couldn't take any more disappointments.

As they reached a clearing, a large yellow house came into view. Sheyna gasped because as many times as she'd come this way, she'd never traveled this far or seen the house before. Who would have ever guessed that on a quiet country lane, just a few easy miles from Sheraton Beach, sat a three-thousand-square-foot farmhouse with white trim on three shaded acres of land? It nearly took your breath away. And then there were the dogwood and pear trees, but what made her heart pound was the white picket fence that surrounded the front of the home.

Jace squeezed her hand, drawing her attention. "What do you think?"

"It's wonderful. It looks like it could use a little work but other than that it's a beautiful house." She looked up at him, her brow bunched inquisitively. "Why do you ask?"

Without answering, Jace took her hand and led her around the side of the house, which was covered with a thick ivy. At the front of the house she saw a Sold sign and her heart sank. This was the house she had always dreamed of.

"Is it okay that we're trespassing?" Sheyna asked as she looked around for any signs of life. "It looks like someone just bought this house."

"It's okay. The owner died years ago and the new owner isn't planning to move in until the house has been renovated," Jace told her as he guided her to the back where a deck ran the entire length of the house.

"It must have been on the market a long time," Sheyna replied as they came to a stop just a few feet from a gazebo at the corner of the yard in what appeared to be a rose garden.

"It was on the market for almost five years."

"I would kill for a house like this! I don't see how it could have possibly been on the market that long."

Jace shrugged. "It's obvious the house needs a lot of work. Not too many people are looking for a fixer-upper, especially this far away from the ocean. You know as well as I do, anyone buying property in Sheraton Beach is looking for beachfront property or condos, not an old farmhouse."

"I guess someone wants it."

"Yep, the man who bought this house is planning to move into this house with his wife and start a new life together."

She turned and gave him a strange look. "How do you know that?"

Slowly he swung around and faced her. "Because I bought it."

Confusion lit her eyes once more. "What? You bought a farmhouse?"

He nodded.

She was more confused than ever. "Why?"

He stroked her face as he spoke. "Because it's where I want to start a life with you as my wife."

She sucked in a breath. "With—"

He caught her just as her knees buckled beneath

her. Carrying her over to the porch, he set her down on an old swing while he explained. "Sheyna, I have been so stupid. Six months ago, I realized that something was happening between us, but instead of exploring those feelings, I chose to run away. I'm tired of running. I love you, precious. I should have told you sooner, but I only figured it out myself a little while ago."

"Y-you love me?" she stuttered.

"With all my heart."

All she could do was sit and stare.

"I can't imagine my life without you. I tried to go back to the way things were, but after our trip to Vegas, I realized that my life just isn't the same without you in it."

Jace slowly got down on one knee and took her hand in his. "Marry me?" he asked.

Sheyna was tongue-tied. "Y-you brought me apple picking so…so you could propose to me?" Tears were running down her face and she was suddenly crying so hard she couldn't speak.

"I wanted you to know that I want to be a part of your world. I want to fulfill all of your dreams." He reached into his pocket, pulled out a ring and slipped the sparkling five-carat diamond onto her finger, then he rose to his feet.

While he waited, his sable eyes searched hers. She loved the man standing in front of her so much. Standing on her tiptoes, she wrapped her arms around his neck and touched her lips to his. "Just remember, marriage to me means forever."

"Does that mean you'll marry me?" he asked anxiously.

"Yes, Jace, I'll marry you. I love you so much!" she exclaimed.

He blew out a breath of relief. "You just made me the happiest man in the world."

Sheyna shook her head. "I don't think anyone could be as happy as I am right now." She squealed as he swung her around in his arms then sealed their future together with a kiss.

Epilogue

The last weekend in June, Jace stood at the front of the church with his brother Jabarie.

He watched the bridesmaids come down the aisle. The first was his sister, Bianca, who looked beautiful in pink. Brenna was the matron of honor. His sister-in-law looked radiant for a woman who just last month had given birth to a baby girl, Arianna Danielle.

At the sound of "The Wedding March," the congregation rose to its feet and turned to face the double doors of Sheraton Beach Baptist Church. The sight of his beautiful bride took his breath away. Sheyna came down the aisle on the arm of her father. She was beautiful in a long white gown, her face radiant with love only for him and it made his heart pound. He had waited all his life for this woman.

Within minutes, they were holding hands and she was standing beside him as they repeated their vows. It wasn't long before he was raising her veil, leaning forward and covering her mouth hungrily.

An hour later they were at the Sheraton Beach Beaumont Hotel where a grand reception was being held. Practically the entire town had come out to share in the festivities.

Sheyna looked across the room at her husband and her heart raced. Jace looked fabulous in a black tuxedo. A sob lodged in her throat. It was still hard to believe that she was now his wife. She couldn't wait for their honeymoon to begin. If she was lucky, during those long eleven days while they cruised to Alaska, they would start their family.

Her eyes traveled across the crowd to Jaden, who was standing on the opposite end of the room. He had been back in Sheraton Beach almost a month now and was spending long hours at the body shop. She followed the direction of his gaze over to Danica who was on the arm of the new high-school math teacher. His brow was bunched with displeasure. Sheyna nibbled thoughtfully on her lower lip. She still didn't know what had happened between the two of them. But the look on his face said Jaden still hadn't gotten over her. Now that he was back in town, it would be interesting to see what happened.

Bianca was standing near the fruit punch talking to Donny, the head of security. The way he kept brushing against her arm said there was more going on than two coworkers having a casual conversation. *No wonder she's been acting so secretive.* Sheyna chuckled inwardly. Her mother-in-law would have a fit if she thought even for a moment her daughter was dating someone she believed to be as common as him.

Sheyna looked up in time to find her handsome husband coming her way and her heart sang with delight. The last eight months had been the best time of her life. Together they had remodeled their dream house and made it everything she'd imagined it to be. As soon as they got back from the cruise, they would officially move in.

Sheyna and Jace finally left the reception and moved upstairs to their suite. They would be catching an early flight tomorrow.

The moment Jace opened the door he swept her up into his arms and carried her over the threshold.

"I love you, Mrs. Beaumont."

She captured his eyes with hers. "Not as much as I love you."

He leaned down and kissed her. She wrapped her arms around his neck and clung to him as he carried her over to the bed. Jace had no doubts about his love for Sheyna. His playboy days were officially over.

ESSENCE **Bestselling Author**

DONNA HILL

SEX AND LIES

Book 1 of the new T.L.C. miniseries

Their job hawking body products for Tender Loving Care
is a cover for their true identities as undercover operatives for
a covert organization. And when Savannah Fields investigates
a case of corporate espionage, the trail of corruption leads
right back to her husband!

Coming the first week of February wherever books are sold.

A dramatic new miniseries from

Bestselling author

DEBORAH FLETCHER MELLO

TO *Love* A
STALLION

Book 1 of The Stallion Brothers

Marah Briscoe intends to use all her charm to keep ruthless
CEO John Stallion from buying her family's ranch. Instead,
she's blindsided by a man as infuriating as he is irresistible!

"Her description of scenes and characters is near perfect.
The sassy dialogue…brings smiles."
—*Romantic Times BOOKreviews* on
Forever and a Day

Coming the first week of February wherever books are sold.

KIMANI™
ROMANCE

The game of love...

PLAYING
for KEEPS

Favorite author

YAHRAH ST. JOHN

Ambitious Avery knows laid-back Quentin isn't her
type—until a crisis drives her into his arms for comfort,
and fierce attraction takes over. Quentin's life leaves no
room for relationships...until he realizes he can't picture
the future without Avery.

Coming the first week of February wherever books are sold.

KIMANI™
ROMANCE

www.kimanipress.com

KPYSJ0550205

A Man Who Has Everything Needs...

More Than a Woman

National Bestselling Author

MARCIA KING-GAMBLE

Anais Cooper put her savvy and savings into creating a charming day spa. The only problem is...her neighbor. Former baseball star turned celebrity real estate mogul Palmer Freeman has declared unofficial war on her business venture. So she decides it's time to add a little sugar to the mix!

Coming the first week of February wherever books are sold.

ARABESQUE®

www.kimanipress.com

KPMKG0830208

"*Eternally Yours*...A truly touching and heartfelt story that
is guaranteed to melt the hardest of hearts."
—*Rendezvous*

USA TODAY Bestselling Author

BRENDA JACKSON

ETERNALLY YOURS

A Madaris Family Novel

Attorney Syneda Walter and fellow attorney
Clayton Madaris are friends—and the last two people
likely to end up as lovers. But things start to heat up
during a Florida getaway and Clayton realizes Syneda
is the woman for him. Can he help her heal old wounds
and convince her that she will always be eternally his?

"Ms. Jackson has done it again!...another Madaris brother
sweeps us off to fantasyland..."
—*Romantic Times BOOKreviews*

**Coming the first week of February
wherever books are sold.**

ARABESQUE®

www.kimanipress.com KPBJ0550208

A compelling short story collection...

New York Times Bestselling Author

CONNIE BRISCOE

&

ESSENCE Bestselling Authors

LOLITA FILES
ANITA BUNKLEY

YOU ONLY GET *Better*

Three successful women find themselves on
the road to redemption and self-discovery as
they realize that happiness comes from within...
and that life doesn't end at forty.

"This wonderful anthology presents very human
characters, sometimes flawed but always
heartwarmingly developed and sympathetic.
Each heroine makes changes for the better that
demonstrate the power of love. Don't miss this book."
—*Romantic Times BOOKreviews* Top Pick on
You Only Get Better

**Coming the first week of February
wherever books are sold.**

KIMANI PRESS™

www.kimanipress.com   KPYOGB1540208